CW01430834

REDEEMING RAFE

BARRETTI SECURITY SERIES #2

SLOANE KENNEDY

CONTENTS

Redeeming Rafe is a work of fiction. Names, characters, businesses, places, events and incidents are either the products of the author's imagination or used in a fictitious manner. Any resemblance to actual persons, living or dead, or actual events is purely coincidental.

Copyright © 2015 by Sloane Kennedy

Published in the United States by Sloane Kennedy
All rights reserved. This book or any portion thereof may not be reproduced or used in any manner whatsoever without the express written permission of the publisher except for the use of brief quotations in a book review.

Cover Images: © Improvisor, Julia Gurevich| Shutterstock.com

Cover Design: Jay Aheer, Simply Defined Art

ISBN-13:
978-1517061784

ISBN-10:
1517061784

REDEEMING RAFE

Sloane Kennedy

TRADEMARK ACKNOWLEDGEMENTS

The author acknowledges the trademarked status and trademark owners of the following trademarks mentioned in this work of fiction:

Call of Duty

ACKNOWLEDGMENTS

A big thank you to Stephanie, Michele, Samantha, Jenn and Fiona for being such amazing Beta Readers!

SERIES READING ORDER

All of my series cross over with one another so I've provided a couple of recommended reading orders for you. If you want to start with the Protectors books, use the first list. If you want to follow the books according to timing, use the second list. Note that you can skip any of the books (including M/F) as each was written to be a standalone story.

Note that some books may not be readily available on all retail sites

Recommended Reading Order (Use this list if you want to start with "The Protectors" series)

1. Absolution (m/m/m) (The Protectors, #1)
2. Salvation (m/m) (The Protectors, #2)
3. Retribution (m/m) (The Protectors, #3)
4. Gabriel's Rule (m/f) (The Escort Series, #1)
5. Shane's Fall (m/f) (The Escort Series, #2)
6. Logan's Need (m/m) (The Escort Series, #3)
7. Finding Home (m/m/m) (Finding Series, #1)
8. Finding Trust (m/m) (Finding Series, #2)

9. Loving Vin (m/f) (Barretti Security Series, #1)
10. Redeeming Rafe (m/m) (Barretti Security Series, #2)
11. Saving Ren (m/m/m) (Barretti Security Series, #3)
12. Freeing Zane (m/m) (Barretti Security Series, #4)
13. Finding Peace (m/m) (Finding Series, #3)
14. Finding Forgiveness (m/m) (Finding Series, #4)
15. Forsaken (m/m) (The Protectors, #4)
16. Vengeance (m/m/m) (The Protectors, #5)
17. A Protectors Family Christmas (The Protectors, #5.5)
18. Atonement (m/m) (The Protectors, #6)
19. Revelation (m/m) (The Protectors, #7)
20. Redemption (m/m) (The Protectors, #8)
21. Finding Hope (m/m/m) (Finding Series, #5)
22. Defiance (m/m) (The Protectors #9)

Recommended Reading Order (Use this list if you want to follow according to timing)
1. Gabriel's Rule (m/f) (The Escort Series, #1)
2. Shane's Fall (m/f) (The Escort Series, #2)
3. Logan's Need (m/m) (The Escort Series, #3)
4. Finding Home (m/m/m) (Finding Series, #1)
5. Finding Trust (m/m) (Finding Series, #2)
6. Loving Vin (m/f) (Barretti Security Series, #1)
7. Redeeming Rafe (m/m) (Barretti Security Series, #2)
8. Saving Ren (m/m/m) (Barretti Security Series, #3)
9. Freeing Zane (m/m) (Barretti Security Series, #4)
10. Finding Peace (m/m) (Finding Series, #3)
11. Finding Forgiveness (m/m) (Finding Series, #4)
12. Absolution (m/m/m) (The Protectors, #1)
13. Salvation (m/m) (The Protectors, #2)
14. Retribution (m/m) (The Protectors, #3)
15. Forsaken (m/m) (The Protectors, #4)
16. Vengeance (m/m/m) (The Protectors, #5)
17. A Protectors Family Christmas (The Protectors, #5.5)

SERIES CROSSOVER CHART

Protectors/Barrettis/Finding Crossover Chart

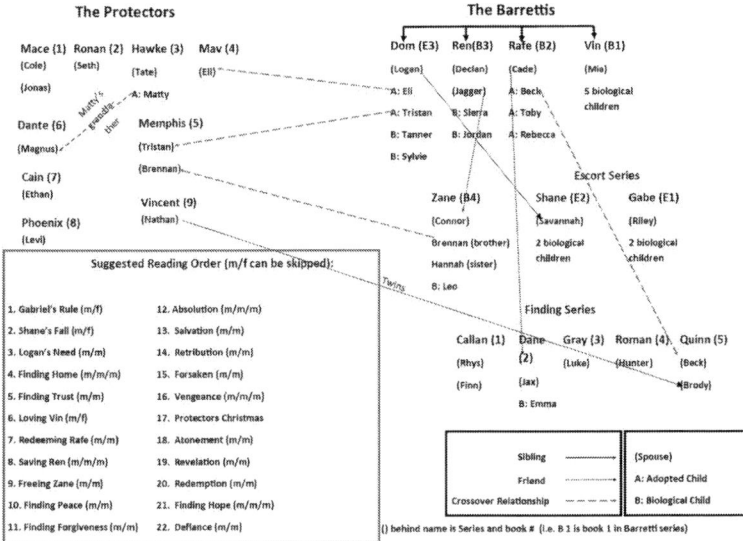

The Protectors

Mace (1) Ronan (2) Hawke (3) Mav (4)

(Cole)   (Seth)   (Tate)   (Eli)

(Jonas)   A: Matty

Dante (6)   Memphis (5)

(Magnus)   (Tristan)

Cain (7)   (Brennan)

(Ethan)

Phoenix (8)   Vincent (9)

(Levi)   (Nathan)

The Barrettis

Dom (E3)   Ren(B3)   Rafe (B2)   Vin (B1)

(Logen)   (Declan) (Cade)   (Mia)

A: Eli   (Jagger) A: Beck   5 biological
                                 children
A: Tristan B: Sierra A: Toby

B: Tanner B: Jordan A: Rebecca

B: Sylvie

Escort Series

Zane (B4)   Shane (E2)   Gabe (E1)

(Connor)   (Savannah)   (Riley)

Brennan (brother) 2 biological 2 biological
                   children   children
Hannah (sister)

B: Leo

Finding Series

Callan (1) Dane   Gray (3) Roman (4) Quinn (5)

(Rhys)   (2)   (Luke)   (Hunter)   (Beck)

(Finn)   (Jax)   Brody

            B: Emma

Suggested Reading Order (m/f can be skipped):

1. Gabriel's Rule (m/f)	12. Absolution (m/m/m)
2. Shane's Fall (m/f)	13. Salvation (m/m)
3. Logan's Need (m/m)	14. Retribution (m/m)
4. Finding Home (m/m/m)	15. Forsaken (m/m)
5. Finding Trust (m/m)	16. Vengeance (m/m/m)
6. Loving Vin (m/f)	17. Protectors Christmas
7. Redeeming Rafe (m/m)	18. Atonement (m/m)
8. Saving Ren (m/m/m)	19. Revelation (m/m)
9. Freeing Zane (m/m)	20. Redemption (m/m)
10. Finding Peace (m/m)	21. Finding Hope (m/m/m)
11. Finding Forgiveness (m/m)	22. Defiance (m/m)

Sibling	(Spouse)
Friend	A: Adopted Child
Crossover Relationship	B: Biological Child

() behind name is Series and book # (i.e. B 1 is book 1 in Barretti series)

TRIGGER WARNING

Listed below are the trigger warnings for this book. Reading them may cause spoilers:

This book contains references to sexual abuse.

PROLOGUE

*C*ade Gamble studied his quarry as the man examined the newspaper in front of him, the coffee the waiter had brought him remaining untouched. When he finally did take a sip, Cade felt his dick tighten at the sight of those firm lips closing over the ceramic edge of the mug. As he swallowed, Cade actually had to stifle a moan because he instantly imagined what it would be like to have his cock shoved down the man's throat as he drank him down the same way he was languidly doing with the coffee. His attraction to the man had surprised him since he was nothing like the men Cade usually went for – soft, eager, submissive and unashamedly gay.

No, this man was anything but those things. He was hard all over with a lean build and toned muscles that filled out the expensive business suit that looked like it had been made just for him. Carefully groomed, dirty blonde hair curled just a little bit above his ears and suggested, when mussed, it would be the perfect length for gripping as Cade thrust into him from behind. A strong, hard jaw was covered with the slightest bit of stubble that would feel rough on Cade's thighs as the man worked that mouth up and down his shaft and the sapphire blue eyes that currently drifted over the paper he was holding would darken to near black with passion as Cade fucked him until he was begging for relief.

Cade shook himself from his thoughts and focused on the newspaper the man was holding. That in itself was unusual since few in this day and age tore themselves away from their phones or tablets long enough to pick up a newspaper, let alone read the whole fucking thing like this guy seemed to plan on doing. The fact that he was supposed to be some computer genius made it even stranger that he'd resort to paper as his medium for learning about what horrible things people were doing to each other in the world today. Cade could have told him it was the same shit they'd done yesterday, the same shit they'd do tomorrow.

The man shifted in his chair as he opened the newspaper and lust clawed at Cade as he watched the long fingers smooth over the paper. Cade searched his pockets for his cigarettes, then remembered Logan had thrown away his last one this morning – a habit that grated on Cade's nerves, but also made a smile tug at his lips. Protecting Logan Bradshaw had been an interesting job from day one and coming to count the man as one of his closest friends had been an unexpected benefit.

Logan's lover, Dominic Barretti had hired Cade to make sure that a threat from Logan's past never got a chance to make another attempt on Logan's life like the one last fall when the man had shot Logan and left him for dead in his burning bar while trying to abduct Logan's sister. Fortunately that threat was gone now, but his friendship with Logan had lingered and the man was determined to get Cade to quit smoking his 'cancer sticks'.

He'd been attracted to Logan too when he'd first started playing bodyguard and the other man had been far from his usual type as well so he was starting to wonder if this was some strange work related fantasy. Of course, Logan hadn't been into him at all since his eyes and heart had belonged to Dom from the get go, but it had been interesting to watch Logan and Dom try to figure out they were meant for each other – something Cade had discovered *after* he'd gotten a brief taste of Logan's perfect lips – lips a lot like the man he'd been following for the past three hours sported.

Cade was seriously beginning to hate the crowded, smoggy streets of L.A., but the man seemed to thrive on them and moved among the hordes of people seamlessly, his confident, powerful swagger on full display as men and women alike moved out of his way, some of them openly gaping at his stunning good looks. He'd responded to neither gender with any kind of sexual interest so Cade still had no idea if the guy was straight or gay or a little bit of both. Not that it mattered to Cade because fucking around on the job wasn't an option and fucking the actual mark was even less of one.

At this point they didn't even know the guy's name – it had been an IP address that had led them to a small, cloistered office smack dab in the heart of the busy city. It had been easy to pick up the mark from there since he was the only one in the small, windowless space. But three hours of endless, pointless errands and numerous stops for coffee had Cade wanting to rip his hair out...or better yet, rip the guy's perfect fucking hair out. There was no way this guy was the one they were looking for – he was just too damn boring, good looks aside. The chances that he was actually the one hacking Barretti Security Group's servers and stealing sensitive information from them seemed unlikely, but there was always the possibility that he would lead Cade to the head of the operation.

Cade took another sip of his own coffee and watched as the man finally closed the newspaper and then pulled out some money and dropped it on the table. Preparing to move himself, Cade was caught off guard when the man suddenly approached him and casually dropped a business card down in front of him. So much for not being made, Cade thought to himself as the guy flashed him a quick smile, the invitation clear in his eyes. Definitely not one hundred percent straight Cade mused as he glanced at the card as he stood to follow. On the front was the symbol of a spade that looked exactly like what one would find in a deck of cards. The back had just an address and a time. So he *had* been made, but not because the guy knew he was trailing him but because the guy thought Cade was looking for a hook-up.

The directive from Dom had been clear – pursue, but don't engage. But what could a little in-depth recon hurt? Maybe a good hard fuck was exactly what was called for.

~

*C*ade glanced at the address on the card as he neared the nondescript building. Nothing about it stood out and if he hadn't followed the guy after he'd left his office, Cade would have guessed the whole thing had been a set up. It still could be, he realized as he knocked on the door. It opened within seconds and he held out the business card to the burly looking bouncer that was covered in tattoos and piercings. The behemoth glanced at the card, then motioned him inside without a word. Cade kept his hands relaxed but at the ready. It would take him just milliseconds to pull the gun he kept tucked in the back waistband of his pants. He followed the bouncer down a short hallway and another door was pushed open. The scent of smoke and sex assaulted him instantly, as did the heat of the writhing bodies before him.

The room was cast in shadows and garish purple and red hangings lined what he guessed were otherwise plain walls. Red velvet furniture with tacky gold trim took up the outer edges of the space and formed a half-circle around a stage where two young men in leather fetish wear were grinding against each other. They were just two of what Cade guessed to be a dozen or so similarly clad men in various states of service to what he assumed were the patrons. The customers were all dressed in black tie and consisted mostly of men, but he did spy a couple of women as well. As he followed the bouncer past each station, he couldn't help but get turned on by the sight of lap dances, blow jobs and in one case, actual full on fucking surrounded by several onlookers. Some type of eerie, string music was playing in the background but it was mostly drowned out by all the moaning and gasping going on.

Cade was led down a back hallway that had no decoration or frill whatsoever – just a single playing card taped to each door. His body tightened as they neared the Ace of Spades card. He stopped in front of the door and the bouncer nodded briefly at him, then went back the way they'd come. Since he wasn't one to give away the element of surprise, he threw open the door without knocking and froze at the sight before him.

His mark had started without him. Blue eyes locked with his as he stepped into the room and closed the door. There were only three pieces of furniture in the room – a small bed with a red and gold bedspread with a tiny nightstand next to it and an oversized armchair in the same exhausting shade of red as the rest of the place. But his eyes weren't on any of those things – they were stuck on those hooded eyes that latched onto his as the young man kneeling at the man's feet bobbed vigorously up and down on the cock Cade wanted to taste now more than ever.

Cade felt his dick harden to uncomfortable new heights as he stepped further inside the room. He couldn't tell much about the man on his knees other than he was young, slim and completely naked. Under any other circumstances, Cade would have been picturing that perfect ass bent over the bed in front of him. But he only had eyes for the man getting his cock sucked and Cade felt an almost irresistible urge to push the kid out of the way and take over because what he didn't see in those dark eyes was the lust he would have expected – the overwhelming passion that would take those eyes from blue to black with one good, hard swallow. No, the man sat there lazily, his big hand gently stroking the bobbing head beneath his fingers, not holding it as he thrust in as deep as he could. It was a fucking waste of a perfectly good mouth.

"Jamie, our guest has arrived," the man drawled as he petted the younger man once more. Jamie released the man's cock and then turned to smile at Cade as his pink tongue came out to lick the taste of the other man from his lips.

Cade moved closer, his eyes on the long, thick cock that lay neglected in the man's lap. He came to a stop in front of the two men and glanced briefly at Jamie who watched him hungrily. One word and he knew that hot little mouth would suck him in to the root.

"Jamie," the man murmured, his eyes on Cade's. "Make our guest feel welcome."

Cade felt Jamie's hands reach for his zipper, but before he could draw it down, Cade snagged him by the hair and forced his head back. Jamie moaned at the sting of pain Cade made sure to inflict and the younger man's eyes glazed over with lust. "Leave us," he said as he released Jamie.

Jamie looked at him with a mix of confusion and disappointment, then glanced back at the man lounging comfortably in the chair. At his slight nod, Jamie stood and hurried from the room.

"I went through a lot of trouble to book Jamie for tonight," the man said casually.

Cade stepped closer so their legs were touching. He glanced pointedly at the other man's cock which wasn't anywhere near as thick and hard as it should have been under Jamie's likely expert touch. "Looks like you should ask for your money back."

A flash of something went through the other man's eyes, but then he chuckled, the sound grating on Cade's nerves because it too, like everything else that had happened since he opened the door, seemed forced. He let his leg brush against the man's and the chuckle disappeared and every muscle in the man's body tensed. His lips drew tight and his eyes darkened. Finally, Cade thought with an inward smirk, a reaction the man hadn't been able to control.

Cade leaned over the chair and put his nose against the man's neck and inhaled his musky scent. He'd expected some type of fancy cologne or aftershave, but it was just the sweet, tantalizing smell of man. It was tempting to taste the skin with his tongue, but the man was drawn so tight that Cade didn't want to risk losing the opportunity to lavish attention on what he really wanted. He pulled back and felt satisfaction go through him at the look of desire and confusion on the other man's expression. Cade dropped his eyes to the man's mouth and wondered if the lips would be as soft as they looked. But no time for that either.

Without any additional warning, Cade dropped to his knees and placed his hands on the man's thighs before lowering his mouth to his crotch and running his tongue along the long, hard shaft. He felt the muscles beneath his fingers bunch and a whisper of air escaped from between the man's lips.

Giving head wasn't something Cade did often so he was surprised at the pleasure that flooded through him when the man's salty flavor exploded over his tongue as he sucked the flared head into his mouth. He circled the tip with his tongue and flicked over the slit, then swallowed more of the hot flesh into his mouth. He felt the man's hand settle over his head, those long fingers skimming through his hair. Petting him much like he'd petted Jamie. But the cock in his mouth was anything but uninterested as it had seemed to be with the younger man. No, it was full and rigid now with just the slightest curve to it. He pulled off and allowed some of his saliva to dribble down the steely length before swallowing more of it down, automatically relaxing his gag reflex so he could take more in. The fingers on his head flexed, then suddenly they were grabbing his hair and pulling hard, forcing Cade to release the delicious piece of meat he'd so been enjoying.

The man tipped Cade's head back far enough so their eyes could connect and Cade saw the indecision and anger there. The man stood, forcing Cade up with him as he maintained his grip on Cade's head. He could have easily gotten free of the brutal hold, but a dark part of him was actually enjoying it. He'd wanted a reaction from the other man and he was definitely getting it.

The man backed him up until Cade hit the wall by the door and then the hand disappeared from his head and closed around his throat. His grip wasn't tight though; in fact, the man's thumb was rubbing back and forth in an almost soothing gesture. But his eyes were cold and dark with furious passion. Cade felt the man's cock brush his through his pants. Then the hand from his throat was moving up and that thick thumb traced his lips which were still damp with the pre-come that had started leaking from the man's cock the moment Cade put his lips on him.

"Open," he heard the man say. The order should've bothered Cade since he was usually the one giving them, but his curiosity was too piqued not to play along so he did. And when that thumb pressed into his mouth, he closed around it and sucked hard, his tongue mimicking what it had been doing to his cock just seconds ago. The man's free hand brushed over Cade's erection.

"Harder," the man ordered and Cade bit down on the fleshy pad of the man's thumb. He was rewarded with a hard rub from the man's hand on his shaft and then that hand was releasing his own dick from his pants and stroking him.

Cade matched the man's pace with his mouth until the thumb was pulled free and the hand closed once more around his throat, holding him in place as the other hand worked its magic. Lust went through him at the display of dominance and he began thrusting shamelessly with his hips. He had no idea what the hell was happening to him; he just knew he needed relief and this man could give it to him. It was a startling realization because no man had ever been the one to control his pleasure before. Cade always took and it was up to his partner to find his own release before Cade finished with him. It made him a selfish son of a bitch, but the supply of men who would take the little he was willing to give was endless.

The hand around his cock slowed to a torturous pace that had him riding the edge of agony and bliss. "Tell me what you want," the man said in a harsh whisper.

"Your mouth on me," Cade answered.

Something in the other man changed with those words and Cade saw the walls come up instantly, shuttered by a mask of hollow indifference. The hand on his dick kept moving, but Cade knew the man had checked out. He was surprised when the man leaned in and placed his lips against his ear. The hand on his shaft stopped, then released him. He felt a warm breath skitter over his ear before the man said in a cold, deadly voice, "Tell my brothers I'll see them soon."

Several long seconds passed as the words sank in, enough time for the man to leave through the door right next to them. By the time he got his painfully hard cock shoved in his pants and opened the door, the man was long gone and the bouncer stood there, arms crossed, a warning look on his face. It took Cade all of twenty seconds to put the man on the ground and hurry down the hall past the orgy in the front room, but he was too late. Rafe Barretti was already gone.

CHAPTER 1

"*I*t was not Rafe!" Dom shouted at him as he threw his glass against the office wall.

Cade had been friends with Dom long enough to know that interjecting at this point wouldn't get him anywhere so he threw back the shot of whiskey and placed the glass on Dom's desk.

"Dom-" Vin said from somewhere behind him.

"No, Vin! No!" Dom yelled as he paced back and forth behind his desk. "It's not him," he repeated, his voice slightly dulled as the truth began to sink in.

Cade didn't need to look behind him to know that Vin had already reached that point and was now nursing his second drink as he fought to accept the new reality that Cade had just thrust upon the two brothers. Rafe Barretti, their long lost baby brother was the same man threatening to destroy not only their business, but their personal lives as well.

At thirty-nine, Vin was the oldest of the four Barretti brothers and had inherited the mantle of patriarch when their father stabbed their mother to death after learning of her affair before taking his own life. The stoic, broody Vin had been just eighteen when they died and had assumed custody of all three brothers. Though at fifteen, Dom had ended up becoming more like a second father to the two younger brothers, Ren and Rafe. It wasn't until a few weeks after the murder-suicide that the truth came to light that Rafe, the youngest, was proof of his mother's infidelity and when his biological father had come calling, eight-year-old Rafe was stolen away from the only home and family he'd ever known.

Cade knew that Dom and Vin had searched for Rafe for years but even with all the resources they'd had available to them after founding Barretti Security Group, neither had ever managed to scrape up even the smallest clue as to Rafe's whereabouts. But now the prodigal brother had returned and from the looks of it, he wasn't in the mood for a family reunion.

"What did he say exactly?" Dom finally asked as he began fixing himself another drink.

"He said he'd see you soon."

"Jesus," Vin muttered.

Dom dumped some more whiskey in Cade's glass before heading to the small seating area in the center of the huge office. Cade grabbed his glass and dropped down onto one of the side chairs while Vin sat stiffly on the expensive white leather couch. Dom continued his pacing.

"Why would he do this?" Dom asked to no one in particular.

Cade had his theories but kept his mouth shut.

"Maybe he's just trying to learn more about us," Dom said desperately.

"He wants to hurt us, Dom," Vin said quietly as he swallowed the rest of his drink. "He's playing with us."

Dom finally sat down in the other chair and put his drink down. He dropped his head in his hands and Cade felt a surge of pity go through him. Of all the Barretti brothers, Dom had been searching for Rafe the longest and as year after year passed with no word, he'd agonized over not knowing what had happened to the little boy he'd promised to watch over.

Cade glanced out the window and settled his gaze on the snow-capped Olympic Mountain range. The only reason he was even in this place, had this life, was because Dom had taken a chance on him. And Cade had just ripped Dom's heart out by telling him the baby brother he'd fought so hard to find was seeking vengeance. Because there was no other explanation for what Rafe was doing.

The first security breach had happened more than two months ago and had included sensitive information relating to Mia Hamilton, the young woman who'd been instrumental in saving the lives of two of Dom's extended family members. It had been Mia's father, Sam, who'd shot Logan the previous year and the reason Cade had been hired to protect the young man. With Logan and Sam's main target, Logan's sister Savannah, out of reach, Sam had gotten desperate and abducted Logan's best friend's girlfriend as well as Eli, a young man Dom had been helping to start a new life. Sam had been seconds from killing his two hostages when Mia intervened and beat him to death with a metal pipe. It was Dom who decided to protect Mia from the subsequent news frenzy by stashing her at Vin's house, unbeknownst to his older brother who'd been out of the country.

Shortly after Vin's arrival back in the States, Dom's tech guys had discovered the first hack and realized details of Mia's brief hospitalization in a mental ward had been stolen, along with the plans to hide her at Vin's house. Everyone had been on edge for weeks after the hack but the information hadn't been leaked and Dom and Vin had written it off as a random act. But then the second breach had happened, then the third. Always subtle and always aimed directly at Dom or Vin and the people they loved. And whatever extra security they installed, the hacker was good enough to get around it.

"He had to know we never stopped looking for him," Dom whispered.

Cade remembered the cold, dead look in Rafe's eyes. "He's not the same little boy you remember, Dom," Cade said as he put the drink down on the coffee table. Cade dug his cell phone out of his pocket and brought up the photo he'd managed to get of Rafe during one of his many coffee breaks. He found himself studying it for a moment, his gaze settling on the soft, perfect lips and the stormy, haunted eyes. God, what it would be like to see those beautiful eyes taken over once more by lust like they'd been for such a brief moment in that dark, quiet room.

"Here," he said as he handed the phone to Dom.

Dom's breath hitched at the sight and he could tell the man was trying to hold back his emotion. Thick fingers skimmed over the picture briefly before Dom reached across the table and handed the phone to Vin.

"Did he say anything else?" Dom asked.

Certainly not anything Cade was going to share. "My guess is he made me right away. You should ask Desi to see if the personnel files were hacked."

"She's still trying to sift through the most recent hack," Vin said as he handed the phone back to Cade.

"What did he get this time?" Cade asked.

Dom stood again, his agitation front and center once more. Vin was the one who spoke up.

"He got the research Dom did on Logan and his friends. And the stuff on Savannah."

Cade sighed as he realized what Vin was saying. Logan and his best friends, Shane and Gabe, had been high class professional escorts for several years and their clients had included women from Seattle's elite upper crust. The damage Rafe could inflict not only to the three men directly but to their former customers as well was mind boggling. Not to mention the details of each man's personal life. Apparently even Savannah's brutal rape at the hands of Mia's father wasn't off limits for the ruthless young man.

"And Ren?" Cade asked, referring to the fourth brother who'd been discovered alive in the Middle East after a year of captivity and torture after his Special Forces team had been ambushed. Vin had managed to bring the damaged man home but his mental stability had become such an issue that Ren had left again rather than risk hurting those around him. But not until after he'd killed a man stalking Mia.

Vin and Dom remained quiet which the same as them answering in the affirmative.

"What the hell are we going to do?" Dom muttered.

Cade slammed the rest of his drink before getting up. "We wait. Whatever he wants, he's just getting started."

~

"*Dom, please, don't let him take me!*"

"*We'll come get you soon, Rafe. I swear!*"

"*Dom, please! Vinny!*"

"*Be brave, Rafe!*"

Rafe jolted awake and lurched up in the bed, his legs tangled in the bedding. He fought to catch his breath as he kicked the covers away and climbed unsteadily to his feet. He stumbled to the window air conditioner that he'd forgotten to turn on before drifting off to sleep and jammed his finger down on the power button. A few seconds of tepid air blew over him before cool air began to drift over his slick skin. Closing his eyes, he began to envision lines of code in his head, the numbers and letters falling perfectly into place as his fingers coasted over the keyboard. As line after line appeared, his breathing began to slow and he felt the constriction in his chest ease. He glanced at the dim numbers on the motel room clock and saw it was after two in the morning. He'd been asleep less than an hour.

Rafe let the cold air wash over him for a few more minutes, then went to the bathroom and turned the shower on. He braced himself and stepped under the cold spray of water, shuddering as the icy liquid rained down on him. Relief went through him as his overheated body began to stabilize and he leaned his head against the grimy tile of the shower stall.

Be brave, Rafe. The words had been spoken by Vin as he and Dom watched Gary Price drag Rafe to his waiting car. It was the last time he'd heard his name too since Gary had changed it. Too fucking exotic, Gary had said. He needed an American name. But he'd never gotten one. No, Gary had just called him 'Boy' instead and since Gary's plans for him hadn't required a real name, he'd kept his stashed away in his mind and waited until his brothers would come to take him home and he'd once again be Rafe Barretti.

Twenty years later and he still didn't have a real name. At least he didn't have to answer to 'Boy' anymore. He'd made sure of that when he was fourteen years old. He probably shouldn't have bothered keeping Rafe as a first name but it was his last link to the mother who'd been taken from him and letting go of the name she'd given him was a line he hadn't been able to cross. The few times he'd even considered it, his mother's voice filtered through his head with stories of the beloved grandfather he'd been named after and he abandoned the idea of being anyone other than Rafe. But there was no Barretti anymore. And there was no other last name either. Only people with families needed last names.

As the tension slowly slid out of Rafe, he bent down and changed the temperature of the water and waited several long seconds for the warm water to drift over him. He was so close. So fucking close. He'd put his plan into motion months ago but now he'd finally get to see the results firsthand. He'd get to watch Dom and Vin lose everything that mattered to them and then he'd close this chapter in his life and build a new one. He'd still be Rafe, but a better one. A Rafe that wasn't still waiting for his brothers to keep their promise and bring him home.

Rafe let his eyes slide closed and was immediately greeted with the memory of firm lips stroking over him as a wet tongue bathed him in warmth. He let his fingers close around his half hard cock and tugged lightly. Cade Gamble. The one wrench in his plan so far. The gorgeous, black haired man had been hard to miss when Rafe hacked the personnel files but he hadn't been concerned that the former mercenary could potentially be the one his brothers would send to investigate him. In fact, when he'd spied the man trailing him that first day a thrill had gone through him at knowing he'd get to face off with the other man who represented everything Rafe despised. Dominant, aggressive, arrogant, take-what-you-want attitude. The guy had all of it rolling off him in spades.

But Gamble had managed to surprise him when he'd dismissed the twink he'd specifically picked out for him and set his sights on Rafe instead. Not that he'd been concerned though. Men like Gamble got so lost in the chase, they never figured out who the hunter really was.

Letting Gamble suck his dick hadn't been part of the plan but he was nothing if not flexible. But he had been caught off guard by his body's reaction to the other man and Gamble had managed to get his cock painfully hard within seconds whereas Jamie had been working him for a good ten minutes before Gamble's arrival. Part of him had wanted to let the whole thing play out since he'd never experienced that level of desire before. But thankfully his common sense had won out and he'd managed to turn the tables on the other man before he'd given in to his baser needs. There'd been a brief resurgence of lust when he'd closed his hands around the man's long, thick shaft but then luckily Gamble had opened his mouth and spoken.

Rafe gave his dick a few vicious tugs and pictured his hand wrapped around Gamble's throat. He hadn't missed the flash of lust that had gone through the other man's forest green eyes as Rafe manhandled him. The bigger man, who had at least three inches on his own 6-foot frame and an additional fifty pounds of pure muscle, could have easily broken free but he'd chosen not to because he wanted what Rafe could give him. He'd wanted Rafe to be in control. An image of Gamble on his knees, shoulders pressed to the floor, hands bound behind his back flashed through his mind. And then Rafe was slamming into him.

"Fuck," Rafe shouted as his release crashed through him without warning and he shot all over the shower wall. "Shit," he muttered as he leaned back against the cold tile and let the water wash away the proof that he might not be as immune to Cade Gamble as he wanted to be...needed to be. Just another obstacle to overcome he told himself as he turned the shower off and reached for a towel. He'd been doing that his whole fucking life.

~

*R*afe watched the dark-haired young man approach him, hand extended. A genuine smile that actually reached his pale blue eyes was plastered across his handsome face. His brother sure knew how to pick 'em. Logan Bradshaw was stunning.

"Mr. Bowers?" Logan said as he shook Rafe's hand.

"Call me Simon," Rafe responded.

"I understand you're interested in learning more about The Sylvie Barretti Hope for Life Foundation," Logan said as he motioned to the small space teeming with people. Most sat behind desks talking on the phone or working at computers. He only saw a couple of kids – street kids likely based on their appearance and demeanor.

"Yes, I've heard your organization is off to a promising start," Rafe said smoothly.

"Well, we're still in the process of trying to get our satellite locations set up – that's where we'll be able to reach out to the kids directly," Logan explained as he led Rafe around the small area. Fresh paint in warm, contrasting colors actually gave the place a homey feel and an area near the back of the building had partitioned walls, probably to offer privacy to the traumatized kids who were foolish enough to seek help in a place like this.

"Impressive," Rafe managed to get out. Dom's lover might be a real looker but he was an utter fool to think his efforts would be well received.

He cast a glance at Logan, expecting to see the man beaming with pride at his so called accomplishment but was caught off guard by the open curiosity on the man's expression. "You don't really believe that, do you, Simon?" Logan asked.

Rafe knew he needed to tread carefully but he couldn't keep the disdain from his voice when he said, "You're an optimist, Mr. Bradshaw. I understand that. But most of the kids you think you're saving are already beyond redemption by the time you get to them. Fancy fundraisers and calling yourself a foundation won't change that. Spend your money on something else – cure cancer or save the environment or whatever else is politically correct at the moment. This," he said as he motioned to the people around them, "is a noble effort but a futile one."

Logan watched him for a moment before chuckling softly. "Cade said you were a cold-hearted bastard."

Rafe stiffened and actually took a step back, his eyes glancing around.

"He's not here," Logan said gently. "Neither are Dom or Vin."

Rafe shifted his eyes back to Logan and his respect for the man went up a notch. A lot of notches actually. "Well played, Mr. Bradshaw."

"It's still Logan. May I call you Rafe or is Simon what you go by these days?" When Rafe didn't answer, Logan continued. "I guess you weren't aware that Cade was able to get a picture of you. That or you were thinking Dom wouldn't share what was happening with me."

It had been the latter.

"I have to admit, I'm a little surprised by the visit, Rafe," Logan said. "Dom tells me you already have everything you need to do considerable damage to him, me, my sister, my friends..."

Rafe stiffened his resolve at the point blank comment. He didn't owe this guy anything and he sure as shit wasn't going to feel guilty.

Logan studied him for a long moment, then nodded his head as if in understanding. "It's not enough to know you're hurting Dom and Vin – you want to see it for yourself."

"Smart and pretty," Rafe said coldly. "I've enjoyed our little chat but since I expect my brothers will be walking through that door at any moment," he said in a clipped tone as looked over his shoulder towards the entrance, "I should be going."

"Here," Logan said as he handed Rafe his phone. "Check my calls, texts. I haven't talked to Dom since this morning."

Rafe ignored the phone and crossed his arms. Logan tucked the phone back in his pocket. "Do you really believe that? What you said about the kids? That they're beyond redemption?" Logan asked as he leaned back against an empty desk.

This was the conversation the guy wanted to have?

"You can't be naïve enough to think what you're doing here will actually change anything? Even if you manage to get one kid off the streets, ten more will take his place. A guy like you shows up offering them a better life?" he quipped. "The ones that don't kill you outright will be figuring out how to roll you for everything you have."

Logan contemplated that for a long time, then finally said, "What if the one kid I do save figures out how to save the ten I couldn't?"

Rafe laughed and shook his head. "Ever the optimist," he muttered.

"Realist, actually," Logan said. "You must know what your brother did for Eli Galvez."

Anger flashed white hot through Rafe and it took everything in him not to react. Eli Galvez had been a teenage prostitute that Dom had taken off the streets, given a better life – the life Rafe should have had. He felt Logan's intense gaze on him and knew the man was watching for some kind of response. Fucker was actually trying to psychoanalyze him?

"So that kid's gonna be the game changer?" he said snidely. "He's going to figure out how to eliminate poverty, abuse, crime, hate? Is he going to walk on water and turn blood into wine too?"

Logan ignored his tirade and his inability to ruffle the young man was pissing him off.

"Eli's the only reason we found Cyrus Hamilton," Logan said. "If you read up on me, you'd know him as Sam Reynolds."

Rafe knew both names. Sam Reynolds had been the alias Cyrus Hamilton had used for years as he raped and murdered more than a dozen women.

"Hamilton was killed by his daughter."

"Yes, but Eli was the one who gave us the information we needed to track him to Summer Hill. How many women were saved because that kid gave your brother a receipt that helped us pinpoint that bastard's location?"

Logan straightened. "Even if all that had happened was Dom giving that kid a better life – giving him a future - shouldn't that be enough? At what point does it cost too much to save even one kid from the hell of having to live in this fucked up world by themselves? Tell me what that number is so I know when to stop trying."

Rafe didn't respond and he was guessing Logan hadn't expected him to. The sight of finally seeing Logan angry should have felt more like a victory but all he felt was a dull emptiness.

"Do whatever it is you're going to do, Rafe. Go tell the world I got paid to fuck my way through Seattle's elite. Tell them my sister was brutally raped by a man I brought into our lives. That my best friend sold himself to try to save his drug-addicted mother and that my other best friend faces his own battle with addiction every day. It won't change anything because you've already won."

That caught Rafe's attention.

Logan smiled sadly and shook his head. "You wanted to hurt Dom, right? What do you think the knowledge that you hate him is doing to him? That you'd rather seek revenge against him and Vin instead of considering forgiveness for whatever happened to you after they lost you?" Logan asked, his voice almost gentle.

Why the fuck wasn't this man railing at him? Why was he talking to him like he was one of the fucked up kids he was trying to save? And they hadn't lost him – they'd let him go!

"They don't get to walk away from this," he said bitterly.

"They're not going anywhere, Rafe. When you've done what you need to do, they'll be waiting for you because they want their brother back."

Fury surged through Rafe and he felt his control begin to fray. He couldn't even manage a parting shot because all he wanted to do was scream at the too calm young man who looked at him with that mix of pity and kindness. Fuck if he needed any of that shit.

He turned and left the building, his long strides eating up the ground as he pushed past the endless throng of tourists near the waterfront. His hands were shaking by the time he got a cab and he was in a full on rage when he threw open the door to his motel. But as he turned to close the door behind him, he caught a glimpse of a dark form standing in the doorway and then something crashed against the side of his head and everything went black.

CHAPTER 2

*R*afe felt pinpricks of light pierce his dry eyes as he tried to force them open. It took several tries before his lids responded but then everything was too bright and his head began to swim as the throbbing pain increased. He let his eyes drift shut again until the stabbing in his temple eased and then he tried again. This time he managed to keep his eyes cracked open just enough to make out a few shapes. It took several long seconds to figure out he was looking at furniture.

"Open," he heard someone mutter just before a hand was pressed to his mouth. He jammed his lips shut when he felt the pills touch his mouth but then his head was yanked back and when he gasped at the pain, the pills slid into his mouth. An instant later water was sloshed into his mouth and he automatically swallowed and the pills easily slid down his throat before he could stop them.

The brutal hold on his hair disappeared and his head lolled forward as water trickled down his mouth.

"Relax, they were just a couple of ibuprofen. I hit you a little harder than I meant to."

Shit, he knew that voice. That deep, smooth, fuck me voice. He forced his eyes open all the way and saw Cade Gamble sitting not ten feet away on a chair that he'd turned around so that his arms were folded across the back of it. Rafe tried to move but then realized that he was bound. But his arms weren't behind him. No, they were stretched high above his head and secured to something that kept him from lowering them. Behind him he could feel a solid, wide object. Some type of beam or post he guessed. A quick look around showed they were in an apartment, a really nice one that was at least a dozen floors up considering the view. Wide open floor plan with dark walls and light furniture. A huge kitchen with black appliances and floor to ceiling windows that showed the water of Puget Sound and the mountains beyond.

His eyes settled on Cade who was watching him with amusement.

"What surprises you more? That I don't live in a piece of shit studio with just a hot plate and a fridge full of beer or that I managed to get you up here without anyone noticing?"

Both but Rafe didn't say that. He was too busy trying to get his breathing under control. It took everything in him not to yank at the piece of plastic pressing his wrists together. Zip ties – the guy had to use zip ties. Not rope or handcuffs or even a fucking tie. God damn zip ties. Panic began to seep into him as he remembered the last time someone had put zip ties on him.

"If you'd done a little more homework on me, you would have known that my merc days paid really, really well. A lot of perks come with having the penthouse but my favorite is the private elevator that goes directly from the garage to this floor. No pesky stops between," Cade drawled.

"So what's the plan Gamble? Jesus, is that even your real name?" Rafe managed to say along with a well-placed chuckle he hoped didn't sound forced. "Let me guess, if I don't give you what you want you're going to fuck me up. Or no, I know, you've got some fancy torture planned for me…"

Cade studied him for a moment, any trace of amusement gone. When the big man rose slowly to his feet, Rafe actually felt the direction of his panic shift from being bound to the dangerous man moving towards him, his pace unhurried. God, he needed to focus on

23

using the man's weaknesses against him – he needed to be the one in control. A thrill went through him when he saw the erection pressing against Cade's jeans. It was something he could use.

"You should have stayed away from Logan," Cade said coldly as he came to a stop in front of Rafe, his long, heavy body just inches away. Rafe had hoped to see some emblem of desire because he could use that to his advantage as well, but all he saw was deadly intent. Cade's dick might be interested but his head sure as hell wasn't. But there were plenty of ways to get the man's brain to catch up to the rest of his body.

"Have a thing for the boss' boy, huh?" Rafe said and a second later his head hit the beam as he instinctively tried to escape the big hand that wrapped around his neck. "Or does Dom share him with you like he did with his wife?"

Any other words Rafe might have said were cut off as fingers pressed down mercilessly on his airway. He actually saw black spots dancing before his eyes when Cade finally let up and he dragged in several harsh breaths.

"I should end you right now you worthless piece of shit," Cade whispered. "I'd be doing your brothers a favor." Cade stared at him for a long moment and then shoved away from him.

"You're lucky they're better men than me," Cade said as he returned to his chair. "Their orders were to leave you alone. Let you do whatever you're going to do." The big man let out a dark, cruel laugh. "They actually think you might come back to them someday."

Rafe willed his heart rate to slow as his brain's attention turned once again to the smooth plastic biting into his wrists. His desperate eyes fell to Cade's lap as he said, "Looks like you have a problem. A couple of them, actually."

He was proud of how cool he'd managed to sound even as his mind began to race. The heat was building inside of him and his breaths began to get shorter and shorter. He was nearly out of time. Letting his eyes drift back up to meet Cade's, he suggested, "Untie me and I can take care of the first one for you. Then maybe we can talk about the rest."

∽

*W*as this guy fucking serious? Cade actually laughed out loud and at Rafe's crestfallen look he laughed harder. So much for thinking the youngest Barretti brother had brains to go with the sinfully gorgeous body.

Snatching Rafe hadn't been in his plans at all until he'd seen the man go into Logan's foundation. There'd been little concern for his friend's physical well-being but Rafe's presence meant that the vengeful young man was intent on witnessing the damage he'd already caused and that even innocent people like Logan weren't immune. So he'd watched and waited and the second Rafe stepped out of that building, he'd made a decision that could end up costing him some of the most important people in his life.

Cade hadn't agreed with Dom and Vin's decision to leave Rafe alone though he understood their thinking. To them he was still the little boy they'd been trying to find for years and Cade knew they truly believed they could get their brother back by letting him work out whatever revenge scenario he had planned. They'd even gotten the go ahead from the many people Rafe's actions would hurt – Mia, Logan, Savannah, Gabe and Riley, Shane – they'd all agreed to let their secrets come to light if it meant giving Dom and Vin back their brother. And the fucking asshole in front of him didn't give a shit that he had a chance to be a part of that kind of family.

Growing up in a double-wide trailer in a small mining town in Alabama with a mean-spirited father and bible toting mother hadn't exactly meant a future rife with options for Cade and he'd known it. Ironically, it was a string of bad choices that had finally gotten him on track when a few strangers saw something good in him and gave him the opportunity he'd needed to clean himself up. And while he'd never managed an emotional connection with any of his sexual partners that would ultimately lead to a meaningful relationship, he'd ended up lucky enough to find a few lifelong friends who had shown him what being part of a family really meant.

Cade settled into the chair and dropped his head down on his arms so he could enjoy the sight of Rafe struggling uselessly against his bindings. But something started to register as he watched Rafe strain desperately against the zip ties he'd attached to the large eyelet secured deep into the foundation beam. Sweat dripped down Rafe's face and Cade could see his shirt was actually starting to stick to his body as the moisture collected beneath the thin material. Rafe's breathing changed dramatically as he began to viciously yank his arms back and forth. Cade waited several long moments for the young man to realize he couldn't get free but instead of settling, his struggles increased.

"Stop," Cade said as he stood up. But Rafe was beyond hearing him as he began gasping in desperation. Suddenly his flailing and writhing stopped and he hung there, his weight causing the plastic to dig into the already damaged skin around his wrists.

"Jesus," Cade muttered as he grabbed his knife from his boot and reached Rafe's sides in four long strides. One quick swipe of the blade against the plastic and Rafe was dropping into his arms.

"Rafe, breathe," Cade said anxiously as Rafe fought to suck in air.

"Hot," he heard Rafe choke out. "So hot."

Cade used the knife to cut away the remaining zip tie around Rafe's wrists but the man's arms flopped uselessly to his sides. Cade half dragged, half carried Rafe to his bathroom and turned the shower on, setting the dial to the coldest temperature. He managed to pull Rafe into the stall and flinched when the frigid water hit them both. He kept his arm wrapped around Rafe's waist to hold him upright and used his other hand to move Rafe's body back and forth so the spray hit him everywhere.

The man was wheezing desperately so Cade leaned him over and pressed his front against Rafe's back and let his free hand settle on Rafe's chest. "Slowly, Rafe. Breathe with me, okay?" he said against Rafe's ear. He felt fingers clutch his.

"In and hold it," he said gently and began counting. "Now out," he said and counted again. He repeated the words over and over and finally felt Rafe's breathing start to match his counting. It took another dozen rounds before Rafe's breathing evened out and the fingers wrapped around his loosened. He felt Rafe sag against him as the cold water continued to rain down on them and he followed the other man to his knees. Cade managed to reach past Rafe to change the temperature of the shower and within seconds the warm water cascaded over them and the shudders that had wracked Rafe's frame began to ease.

Cade let his arm wrap back around Rafe and before he realized what he was doing, he skimmed a soft kiss over the back of Rafe's neck. Rafe's hand closed over the hand Cade had pressed to the man's chest and a shot of longing went through him when he felt Rafe's fingers intertwine with his.

Forcing himself to pull back, Cade put space between their bodies. The other man didn't follow and when Cade pulled his hand free, Rafe remained on his knees, head hung. Broken. Cade turned off the shower and got out to grab several towels from the closet.

He pulled Rafe gently to his feet and began working the buttons on his shirt free. He could tell Rafe was aware of what was going on but the man remained mute and didn't protest as Cade pulled the shirt off, then dragged the slacks down each leg. The underwear followed but Cade ignored the flaccid cock and ran a towel over Rafe's body. When he turned Rafe to dry his back, he froze at the sight of dozens and dozens of scars along his back and ass. Bile rose in his throat but he forced himself to finish the task at hand. He wrapped a dry towel around Rafe and tugged him into the adjoining master bedroom and sat him down on the edge of the bed. The man was so withdrawn that Cade didn't even bother to tell him not to move when he left the room. He returned within a minute and shoved a glass of orange juice into Rafe's hand.

"Drink it," he urged. "All of it."

Rafe swallowed the entire contents down in a few swallows and then just held the glass numbly in his hand. Cade pulled it free and then got Rafe settled beneath the covers. Rafe's hollow eyes stared straight ahead and Cade fought back the urge to run his fingers over the man's cheek. God, he just wanted a response – any response. But instead Cade turned and left the room, pulling the door closed behind him. Why the hell hadn't he just listened to Dom and left the man alone?

~

*R*afe glanced around the empty apartment in disbelief. It had to be a trick. No way would Cade just let him walk away. He'd been surprised to find his clothes freshly laundered and sitting on the end of the bed when he'd finally woken up. A glance at the clock had shown it was nearly seven at night. He'd spent more than half a dozen hours passed out in his enemy's bed. And instead of waking up to threats or snide comments about his humiliating display of weakness, he was completely alone. No note, no locked doors, no warnings, nothing. What the hell?

Rafe didn't linger as he left the penthouse and took the stairs down to the main floor. It took only minutes to hail a cab and then he was back at his crummy hotel room. There was still no sign of Cade or his brothers so he decided not to press his luck and packed his shit together. Another cab took him to an equally rundown motel in a less than stellar neighborhood and by the time he was settled in the room, his nerves were completely frayed. He checked all his belongings for any kind of tracking device and then searched his laptop for any foreign activity. Nothing. Everything was exactly as he'd left it.

Frustration went through him as he tried to figure out what was going on. He didn't believe for a second what Logan and Cade had said about his brothers leaving him alone to do what he wanted. No man would lie down and allow a stranger to come in and destroy everything he loved.

Rafe's head began to pound and he quickly closed the laptop. Maybe his plan to bear witness to his brothers' downfall wasn't worth it. God knew he couldn't risk another encounter with Cade. By now the man had probably told Dom and Vin about his crippling panic attack. And he'd known the second Cade had seen the marks on his back because the warm, firm stroking that had been relaxing him as

Cade ran that soft towel over his body had stopped the minute Cade had turned him around. And that kiss...

It had been brief and soft and barely there but the reaction would have been the same if Cade had kissed him on the mouth. His whole body had warmed at the gentle caress and he'd been unable to stop himself from lacing his fingers through the strong, blunt ones that had been splayed over his chest. Rafe reached behind his neck and skimmed his fingers over the skin Cade had touched. Shit, even Cade's mouth on his cock hadn't messed with his head like this.

Rafe dropped his hand and opened the computer again. He needed to end this. All the emails were queued and ready to go. One push of a button and Dom and Vin's reputations would be shredded, the truth about their loved one's pasts revealed. The press, the firm's clients, everyone would see that his brothers used smoke and mirrors to build themselves up to be better men than they were. He could go back to L.A. and put this part of his life behind him. The fucking nightmares and panic attacks would stop and he'd never have to hear his brothers tell their lies again.

$\approx$

*C*ade watched Rafe shift uneasily on the bench as his eyes darted nervously around him and then back at the revolving door that led into the building where Barretti Security Group was housed. At this point Cade had no idea if Rafe was trying to avoid seeing Dom or Vin or actually hoping they'd come through the door so he could catch a glimpse. From his position in the park across the street, Rafe was inconspicuous and it was unlikely that his brothers would even notice him if they did happen to exit through the front door of the building. Whatever Rafe was up to, he'd been doing it for three days now. The same exact routine from the moment he left the dive he was currently staying in to the moment he went back and hid himself away in the tiny room. Logan's foundation was always first and Rafe used the alley across the street as cover. Dom's apartment was next since it wasn't far from Logan's place of business. Then came the office building and it was always followed up with a cab ride to the northern part of the city where Vin owned a house.

Cade leaned back in the seat of his non-descript sedan. Tracking the man was much easier this time around since he'd planted the tracking device in Rafe's phone. He'd known the man would easily be able to tell if his phone had been hacked so he'd gone old school and used a nifty little tracking device that a friend from the FBI had given him. The chip had been easy to hide within the phone's motherboard so his only real worry had been that Rafe would ditch the phone all together. So far so good because the way Rafe was constantly looking around, he was clearly still suspicious.

Rafe jumped up from the bench and began walking towards the street. Cade didn't need to glance at his watch to see that it was nearly three o-clock in the afternoon. He took his time easing into the early afternoon traffic. It was always this last leg of Rafe's journey that confused him most since Vin's house was so fortified with security that Rafe couldn't get more than a hundred feet from the iron gate that was surrounded by security cameras. There was no place to blend in either so Rafe usually sat in the cab at the end of Vin's street and the only view of the house he would have had would be the roof and maybe a window or two. But he'd sit there for more than an hour before directing the cab back to the city and then he'd end up back in front of Dom's apartment where he spent the rest of the evening drinking coffee in the café across the street.

Once they were back in the city, Cade parked his car two blocks from the coffee shop and made his way through the crowd of people until he reached the edge of the park next to Dom's building. He had a clear view of Rafe who was seated in the patio area, his fingers tapping nervously on what Cade guessed was his third cup of coffee by now. There was a newspaper in front of him but it remained untouched. To the casual observer Rafe looked like any other tourist or regular and the only thing that set him apart was his good looks and confident demeanor. But Cade didn't miss the many times Rafe nervously ran his hand through his hair or checked his watch. His expression was drawn tight and the agitation was clear in his shifting gaze.

Guilt went through Cade when he saw Rafe pull down one of his shirt sleeves that had ridden up. There were still red marks where the zip ties had cut into Rafe's skin as he'd fought them. As infuriated as he'd been with Rafe, he hadn't meant to truly harm him. Yeah, knocking the guy out had been a necessary means to an end but that was supposed to have been the worst of it. He sure as shit hadn't planned to send the guy into a debilitating panic attack. And the scars...the fucking scars.

He'd seen marks like those before – had felt the same bite of leather himself. Whatever had happened to the youngest Barretti after he'd been stolen from the protection of his big brothers appeared to have left even worse scars on the inside than the ones on the outside and any justification Cade had felt in going after the guy to protect Dom and Vin and the rest of his second family had dissipated. Maybe Rafe Barretti did need his brothers to be there to welcome him home, no matter what kind of damage the young man inflicted before he got there.

Cade saw Rafe stiffen and he instantly went on alert. He glanced across the street and saw Dom and Logan walking hand in hand down the sidewalk, their heads lowered as they spoke softly to one another. Cade looked back at Rafe and saw the man was on the move, his dark gaze latching onto his brother as if he was some type of prey. With Rafe's attention engrossed by his unsuspecting brother, Cade was able to keep the distance between them pretty minimal and when he saw Rafe start to go into the restaurant after Logan and Dom, he quickened his pace and reached Rafe as he paused just outside the entrance.

He grabbed Rafe's arm and snapped "not one word" when Rafe opened his mouth to argue. It took just seconds to drag Rafe deep into the alley next to the restaurant and shove him back against the wall. They were hidden from the foot traffic by two huge dumpsters and though the smell left something to be desired, the privacy was what Cade had been looking for.

"So now the plan is to humiliate your brother in person?" Cade snapped.

Rafe was breathing heavily, his sapphire eyes glittering with anger and something else. Lust – hard and raw. Desire slammed through Cade like a bullet as his eyes fell to Rafe's slightly parted lips. This was the man he remembered from that night so long ago in the club. Powerful, confident, in control. But there was a hint of vulnerability too and he knew Rafe was waiting for him to decide what would happen next. He'd seen this man at his weakest and Rafe was expecting him to use it against him.

"Fuck it," he growled as he leaned down and sealed his mouth over Rafe's. He'd meant the kiss to be harsh and demanding – proof that he had the power in this moment but the second the soft lips parted beneath his, all thoughts of punishment fled and he eased back so that his tongue could gently brush over Rafe's. The man's mouth was amazing and the feel of his slick tongue greeting his own had Cade pressing his body into Rafe's until the wall at Rafe's back gave Cade the leverage he needed to mold their bodies so nothing between them was left untouched. He let his hands close over Rafe's wrists and brushed his thumbs across the bruised skin there before dragging his arms up to each side of his head. When he fisted his hands around Rafe's, the other man's fingers instantly intertwined with his.

His dick felt like a steel pipe beneath his jeans but he was enjoying the feel of Rafe's hands clinging to his too much to release them so he settled for rubbing their groins together. But soon that wasn't enough and he let go of one of Rafe's hands and fumbled between their bodies. He said a little prayer of thanks when his hand easily slipped past the waistband of Rafe's slacks and closed around the thick shaft that was already slick with moisture.

Rafe cried out at the contact and turned his head to the side as Cade began stroking him. He fastened his mouth over the pulse point on Rafe's neck and sucked hard as he tightened his grip and began pumping his own cock against Rafe's body. Moans spilled from Rafe's mouth as he began thrusting into Cade's hand and Cade managed to fuse their mouths once more as Rafe's desperate cries grew louder. He felt a hand slide into his hair and then Rafe was taking over the kiss, holding Cade's head the way he wanted it as he thrust his tongue in and out of Cade's mouth in tandem to Cade's merciless drags on his dick. The only warning Cade got of Rafe's orgasm was the tightening of Rafe's grip in his hair and he managed to close his mouth over Rafe's just as he let out a loud shout. Warm heat slid down his hand and it was enough to send him over the edge. He jammed his hips against Rafe's once more and then groaned as his seed flooded the inside of his underwear and seeped into his jeans.

Cade stroked Rafe's softening dick gently as they both struggled to catch their breath. He finally pulled his hand out of Rafe's pants and then licked off the evidence of Rafe's orgasm as the other man watched him. Rafe ran his tongue along his lips at the sight and Cade took that as an invitation and kissed him again. He let his palms slide down to cup Rafe's tight ass and dragged the man against his still half hard cock.

"I need to be inside you," Cade groaned against Rafe's lips. "Come back to my place with me."

Cade dipped in for another kiss but Rafe suddenly shoved him back. "Get the fuck off me! No one fucks me," Rafe snapped. "No one!"

The man's rage was palpable and Cade remained silent as Rafe pushed off the wall and strode down the alley. He was glad to see that Rafe didn't turn back towards the restaurant when he got to the main street. As for the rest of the shit that had just happened, he had no fucking clue.

CHAPTER 3

*R*afe scrubbed desperately at the stain in his slacks, wishing like hell that removing the proof of what he'd just allowed to happen would eliminate the act as well. He cursed himself for the thousandth time as he flung the pants aside and ripped off his underwear. A quick shower removed the rest of the evidence from his body but no amount of brushing his teeth would get rid of Cade's taste and how it had mixed with the salty, bitter flavor of Rafe's own come.

Watching the man lick Rafe's juices from his long, thick fingers had gotten Rafe hard again and when those big palms had cupped his ass, a thrill had gone through him at the rough contact. The whole encounter had proven that Rafe had little to no control over his body around Cade and that was unacceptable. No man would ever hold that kind of power over him again and the fact that Cade had just assumed that Rafe would bend over and take whatever Cade gave him was a good reminder that that was all he was to the bigger man – a piece of ass.

Rafe wrapped a towel around his waist and went to his computer. He was done – this was going to end tonight. He should have pushed the button days ago but something inside of him had needed more. He'd worried that maybe a few clicks of the mouse wouldn't be enough so he'd spent the next day doing more recon. Not because he was feeling any kind of doubt, he'd told himself. No, he'd needed to finish his plan and bear witness to the lives he was about to change. He'd only started at Logan Bradshaw's foundation because it was closest to his motel, not because he felt some inexplicable draw to the place or the naïve young man running it. And he'd wanted to see Dom and Vin's homes and business so that he could have a good 'before' image to go with the 'after'. It hadn't mattered if he would have happened to have seen his brothers. If he had, it would have been pure circumstance and nothing else.

God, when had he become such a bad liar that he couldn't even fool himself? His entire life had been about manipulating those around him to get what he needed. It had all been done to bring him to this point and now he was reduced to trying to convince himself that his insane behavior the past three days had been part of the plan. And what the hell kind of explanation did he have for what had just happened with Cade? In an alley. Behind a fucking dumpster.

Rafe dropped his head in his hands. He'd like to say that the unex-pected sight of Dom with his young lover had been the cause but it would be yet another lie. It was true that seeing his brother had set something off in him and he'd followed the two men in a fit of fury, but what had happened with Cade would have happened either way because his body wanted the other man, pure and simple. Not once in his twenty-eight years had sex been about pleasure for him and he'd finally accepted that it never would be. It hadn't even become a biological need anymore - at least not beyond what his own hand could do for him. And now this. An undeniable craving for a man bent on taking from Rafe what he wanted – his body and his surrender. Just like all the fucking others.

Rafe flinched when a heavy pounding rattled the door to his room and he closed his eyes because he knew exactly who it was. It didn't surprise him in the least that Cade knew exactly where he was. More pounding had Rafe rising to his feet. He steeled himself for the inevitable battle and yanked the door open. But the sight of Cade in his tight black T-shirt and still stained jeans silenced any forthcoming words. Cade looked exactly like Rafe was feeling – confused, frustrated, angry...needy. Cade didn't speak or enter the room. He just stretched his arms along the doorframe and waited. His eyes held Rafe's and Rafe knew he was being given a choice. He finally did the only thing he could do – he took several steps backwards.

Cade was on him before the door even slammed all the way shut and his towel hit the floor as Cade's tongue thrust between his lips. Desire shot through him as Cade's tongue swept into his mouth and licked over every surface. Big arms wrapped around him and skimmed over his back, blunt fingertips pressing into his heated flesh. But when a hand drifted over his ass, he froze and pulled back.

"I can't-" he started to say but Cade stopped his words with a hard kiss before drawing back. Cade's hand grabbed his and pulled it behind him so that Rafe's fingers were resting on the firm muscles of Cade's ass.

"Whatever you want, Rafe," Cade whispered before kissing him again.

Disbelief went through Rafe as Cade's words sank in. Cade dragged his shirt off and Rafe's fingers moved on their own and began tracing the tattoo that covered much of Cade's left pectoral muscle. Cade's skin rippled and flexed beneath his touch and he heard the other man's breathing pick up as Rafe trailed his hand down over the six pack abs to rest just above the waistband of his jeans. He let the hand he still had on Cade's ass drift up to his lower back and then stopped at the feel of cold metal. Cade stiffened when Rafe carefully pulled the handgun free of Cade's pants but he just reached past Cade and placed it on the small table next to his computer. And then Cade was kissing him again as Rafe fumbled with the fastenings of Cade's pants.

Rafe felt a fist close around his cock and he stifled a moan as the rough skin of Cade's palm dragged over his sensitive length. Hunger went through him and he grabbed Cade's jaw to force the man to stop kissing him. "Get me ready," he said huskily and felt his whole body draw tight when Cade dropped to his knees without any hesitation.

A hot mouth replaced the fingers on his shaft and he watched

Cade's slick tongue make its way down to his balls. One testicle was drawn into liquid heat, then the other and then Cade was sucking his crown into his mouth and flicking his tongue over the slit.

"Yes," Rafe snarled as he pushed his cock deeper into Cade's welcoming warmth. He let Cade give him a few sucks, then pulled his dick out and ran the head all around Cade's parted lips, his pre-come glistening on the supple skin. He shoved his cock back into Cade's mouth and rammed it down his throat and pulled back only when Cade began to gag. But then fingers closed around his ass and Cade was drawing him further in as he began to work Rafe's dick over until Rafe was sure he would explode. "Enough," he bit out as he slipped his cock free of Cade's tight, suctioning grip.

When Cade started to rise, Rafe put a hand on his shoulder. An inner darkness swept through him as he used his hand to press Cade down until his hands were braced on the floor. He knew he should take Cade on the bed but he needed to remember this for what it was – a good hard fuck that they both needed to get each other out of their systems. The bed was soft and the last thing he wanted to be around this man was soft.

Cade didn't utter any protest when Rafe dropped into position behind him and yanked his pants and underwear the rest of the way down. He ran his hands over the perfect globes of Cade's ass, then parted them and settled his gaze on the small opening twitching in anticipation. As badly as he wanted inside, he wanted a taste too and he bent down to lick his way around the wrinkly skin before teasing the hole with the tip of his tongue.

"Fuck, yes," Cade moaned as he pressed back against Rafe's probing tongue. Rafe leaned back enough to dribble saliva onto the opening as it flexed and then he sucked on it hard. Cade cursed again and he felt the man shift beneath him, likely reaching for his cock.

Rafe reared back and swatted Cade's hand from his dick and used his own to give Cade a few light tugs.

"My wallet," Cade whispered as he glanced back at Rafe. Rafe shuddered at the unbridled lust in Cade's eyes and he had to force back the emotion that was welling deep inside of him. It was just fucking, he reminded himself sharply as he searched out Cade's wallet and found a condom and a packet of lube. His fingers shook as he rolled the condom on and he tried to ignore Cade's whimpers as he worked the lube into his body.

He knew he should prep Cade more but he was already on the verge of losing it so he rose up and pressed his cock between Cade's cheeks and pushed. Cade bore down on him and moaned again as Rafe began to breach him. The pressure and heat on his dick was nearly his undoing and when he finally sank all the way in, he quickly pulled out and slammed back in again. Cade grunted but pushed his hips back on the next thrust. Rafe shuddered as Cade's body sucked him in on every down stroke and tried to keep him there when he pulled out. The pace he set was brutal but Cade's groans told him the other man was right there with him.

Rafe looked down to watch his cock glide smoothly in and out of Cade's body and he instantly wished the latex barrier gone so he would know what every part of Cade felt like. A tingle went through him and he glanced up to see Cade watching him over his shoulder, his eyes shining with passion. Something inside of Rafe uncoiled at the sight but he shoved it away and pressed his hand down on Cade's shoulders, forcing his upper body to lay flush with the floor. He grabbed both of Cade's wrists and pinned them behind Cade's back and held them there with one hand while he braced the other on Cade's hip and began hammering into him mercilessly.

Rafe knew he was being too harsh but Cade's complete submission had shredded what little control he had left. Since he had no way to brace himself, Cade's cheek and shoulders scraped back and forth over the hard floor with every one of Rafe's brutal thrusts and Rafe knew he should release Cade's hands. But he needed this too badly and he was too close. And it was what Cade wanted, he reminded himself. The man was here to get off and that was it. It wasn't about emotion. Hell, it was barely even about feeling good. It was about coming hard and long and nothing more.

With that in mind, Rafe ignored the ridiculous desire to lean over Cade's body and savor the warmth of their flesh pressed together.

Instead he reached around Cade's hips with his free hand and viciously stroked Cade's cock. Cade's grunts increased every time Rafe slammed his hips forward and within a minute he was screaming in pleasure as his orgasm ripped through him. The feel of Cade's release spilling into his hand had Rafe's body unfurling as the pressure exploded and he shot over and over into the condom as Cade's inner muscles rippled around him. Before he could stop himself, Cade's name tore free of his lips and then he was slumping over Cade's back, the man's arms still between them.

~

*C*ade closed his eyes as his body continued to convulse every time Rafe rocked into him. His arms burned from the angle Rafe had been holding them in for so long and the added weight of Rafe's body didn't help, but there was no way in hell he was going to move while his sated body continued to enjoy the aftershocks of what Rafe had done to him. He lowered his hips to the floor and was surprised when Rafe's hand stayed on him and continued to massage him gently. Their bodies were touching nearly everywhere now and Cade just wished it could have been like that from the moment Rafe had pushed him to the ground. He didn't give a shit that they'd ended up on the floor instead of the bed, but something about the position had him wondering if it had been Rafe's way of keeping them disconnected as much as possible.

He'd had no intention of coming to the motel after the episode in the alley, especially after Rafe's admission that he would only top. But Cade had ended up here anyway even though the reason why and what it meant had scared the hell out of him. The reason was simple – he was fast becoming obsessed with the damaged man who only knew how to lash out. The what it meant part was harder. It meant he'd have to give up the one thing that had always protected him in his sexual encounters. Control.

Cade had known from the time he was a pre-teen that he was gay and his darker needs had always led him to be the one in charge of his and his partner's pleasure. Even during his first encounter at fourteen with a high school senior, he'd ended up topping. There'd never been any desire to submit to someone else or let someone else decide if and when he would find his release. The one time he'd finally given in had been when he was a Private in the army and the Staff Sargeant he'd been fucking on the side for the better part of a month had convinced him to try it. The experience had been a painful one and his only one. There'd been a part of him that had enjoyed the thrill of being taken but the actual act had failed to live up to the hype and there'd been no one since that he'd even considered it with.

Until Rafe.

It had been the memory of the lust that had consumed him when Rafe had dominated him for those brief moments in the club after their first meeting that had him getting out of his car and knocking on Rafe's door. As much as it had terrified him to give up so much of what inherently made him who he was, his instinct had told him that Rafe wouldn't hurt him and that anything the man did to him would ultimately be about pleasure, not pain. And he'd been one hundred percent right.

The feel of Rafe restraining him, holding him immobile, hadn't scared him for even a moment – it had just heightened all the sensations that had bombarded him since all he could do was feel. Even with the emotional distance that Rafe had maintained, the other man had still taken care of him in the end and Cade had come harder than he ever would have thought possible.

Cade felt Rafe shift above him and his sore ass clenched when Rafe finally withdrew from him and stood. Disappointment went through him when Rafe left him on the floor and disappeared into the bathroom. He hoped maybe he'd return with a washcloth to clean him off but when he heard the shower come on a coldness settled into his gut, replacing the warmth that had flowed through him as his orgasm waned. He almost laughed out loud when he realized how many times he'd been the one getting up and walking away. Karma really was a bitch.

Cade dragged himself to his feet and reached for some tissues on the nightstand and cleaned himself up as best he could. He pulled his pants up and sat on the edge of the bed as he swiped his shirt off the floor. His eyes drifted up to where his gun sat on the table and then his gaze settled on the open laptop. Dozens and dozens of emails were sitting unsent in the outbox of the email program and they all had the same subject line. *Barretti.* That was it – nothing more. One word that was enough to get people to open the email. The Barretti name was well known throughout Seattle not only because of Dom and Vin's successful company, but because of their role in the downfall of one of the worst serial rapist and murderers the Pacific Northwest had ever seen. From the looks of things, Rafe had finally decided to take the last step in his plan.

Cade heard the shower stop and he knew that was his cue.

~

*H*e was such a fucking coward. Not to mention an insensitive asshole for leaving Cade lying on the floor like a piece of trash. Shame flooded through Rafe as he yanked on the slacks he'd tossed on the floor after his efforts to clean them before Cade's arrival. They were still damp and it took him a few seconds to work them up his legs. It gave him the time he needed to work up the courage to go into the other room. If he was really lucky, Cade would already be gone.

But he wasn't. He was sitting on the edge of the bed working his shirt down the ripped muscles of his back – the one Rafe had had a perfect view of as he'd driven in and out of Cade's beautiful body. And he hadn't let himself explore any of it, including the intricate tattoo that spread out across his shoulders.

Rafe saw Cade reach for his gun and it was then that he realized his computer was open and the emails he'd planned to send before Cade's arrival were in plain view. He braced himself for the torrent of anger that he knew Cade would release on him on behalf of his brothers but watched in stunned silence as Cade stood, grabbed his gun and tucked it into the waistband of his pants and left the room. Not even one look in his direction.

Rafe leaned back against the doorframe of the bathroom and felt his knees buckle as self-disgust went through him like a knife. He'd treated Cade no better than a whore. He'd become one of the very men he despised. As he sank to his ass he glanced at the computer once more. It was time to end this and move on.

~

*R*afe welcomed the light rain as it cooled his skin. It would have been smart to have the cab drop him off in front of his brother's restaurant but he knew he'd need the last couple of blocks to try and settle his nerves. He'd hoped to do this in a more private setting but a quick hack of Dom's secretary's calendar had showed that he was scheduled to be at his restaurant tonight. It hadn't come as a surprise to find that Dom owned an Italian restaurant. He and Rafe had always been the ones at their mother's side when she was cooking her rustic, old-fashioned pasta dishes. In truth, Dom had been helping to cook while Rafe had been the glorified taste tester, a role any little kid that worshipped his mother and idolized his big brother would have been willing to take on to spend more time with them. In the few weeks he'd had with his brothers before Gary had come for him, Dom's cooking had managed to bring back their mother for a few precious moments as they sat down to dinner as a family of four instead of six.

It was well past eight and the sun had just finished setting by the time Rafe stood in front of the glass door with *Barretti's* etched into it. He was surprised by the lack of activity at the still early hour but it didn't matter since this was going to be a quick in and out thing. Then he'd get his ass to the airport and back to L.A. where he could figure out who he was going to be going forward.

Rafe sucked in a breath and marched through the door. He was already more than halfway in the main room when he realized the place was completely empty except for one group of people against the far wall. Several tables had been moved together and he counted at least a dozen people sitting with glasses raised, their attention on Dom and Logan who sat at the head of the table along with a young man and woman that Rafe recognized as Logan's sister, Savannah and her boyfriend, Shane.

"To the happy couple," someone said. Horror went through Rafe as he lifted his eyes and saw a banner above the table that read, *Congratulations on Your Engagement.*

It was a party. A fucking engagement party. Tears stung Rafe's eyes at the betrayal he hadn't seen coming. All the torment his brothers had supposedly been feeling since his arrival and the reality was that he wasn't even a blip on their radar. Life was moving on as if he weren't even here. Dom wasn't even broken up enough to postpone getting engaged to his lover.

"Rafe," he heard in a horrified whisper. Every head swung around but it was only Dom's stunned eyes that he saw as the expensive glass in his brother's hand slipped from his grip and shattered into a thousand pieces on the floor.

~

*C*ade stood at the sight of Rafe and started to go around the table when he saw the agony flash over the young man's features.

"Oh my God," someone whispered.

"Rafe?" he heard Dom say in a hoarse voice and then Dom was covering his mouth with his hand as his eyes brightened with tears. Vin had stood too and Cade saw him reach blindly for Mia who was sitting next to him. The young woman grabbed his hand and held it tight as both men stared mutely at the brother they hadn't seen in twenty years.

Cade ignored everyone along with the implication of what he was doing and hurried to Rafe's side.

"Rafe," he began gently but Rafe put out his hand and took several steps away from him. Tears were streaming down his face as he took in the scene in front of him and Cade knew instantly what the young man was thinking.

"Rafe, the party is for Savannah and Shane. They got engaged a month ago but this was the first chance Shane's parents could fly out to celebrate," Cade said as he motioned to the two older people sitting next to Shane.

Dom came around the table, glass crunching beneath his feet. "Oh God, thank you," Dom said as he began closing the distance between him and his brother.

"Don't you fucking touch me!" Rafe snarled as Dom neared him and the viciousness had Dom freezing where he stood.

"Rafe, please," Vin said softly as he eased up behind Dom.

Suddenly Rafe flung something at Dom and somehow he managed to catch it. It was a small flash drive. Rafe looked around the room and shook his head before whipping back around to look at his brothers with disdain. "It's all there," he snapped as he motioned to the flash drive. "Go ahead and keep hiding behind your lies. I'm done!"

Rafe turned to go.

"I tried, Rafe! Damn it, I tried!" Dom yelled as he took a few steps forward.

Rafe stopped but didn't turn around.

"I swear on my life, Rafe, I never stopped looking," Dom cried brokenly.

When the young man turned to face his brother there was no pity or understanding, just rage.

"When did you try, Dom? When you were marrying your wife? Or starting your business? Or counting the millions of dollars you were making?" Rafe bit out. His eyes fell on Logan. "Or when you were pursuing someone else a month after the supposed love of your life died?"

Dom reared back but Rafe was merciless.

"How long after you let that bastard take me before you were laughing, loving, living? Because I never did any of those things again."

"Rafe," Vin tried to interject.

"'Be brave, Rafe.' That's what you said, Vinny. You remember?"

Vin nodded weakly.

"I tried. I tried so fucking hard. I was brave when Gary knocked me around for crying too much in the car as we were driving away from you. I was brave when he told me my mother was a fucking whore who got what she deserved. And I was brave when he sold me to a trucker for a tank of gas and a six pack at the very first truck stop we hit."

Rafe's voice cracked and Cade tried to reach for him but he ripped himself away. "And I was fucking brave when that sick fucker pushed me down in the back seat of his rig, stuffed a sock in my mouth and shoved his dick into my ass over and over before handing me back to Gary and telling him I was worth every penny."

Horrified gasps went through the small group of people and Cade watched the denial flash across Dom's features for a split second before the truth really hit him. He shook his head and Cade was sure the word "no" kept falling from his lips as he was suddenly consumed with gut wrenching sobs. Logan was at his side instantly. Silent tears streaked down Vin's face and Cade wasn't sure if he even noticed when Mia wrapped her arms around him.

"I was brave because I knew my big brothers would come for me because they promised me they would. Two years! Two goddamn years and countless men before I gave up. Before I stopped being brave. Before I finally realized you weren't coming to get me!"

Cade saw Dom slowly sink to his knees. He kept shaking his head back and forth but there was no sound coming from him anymore besides harsh, dragging breaths as he tried to pull enough oxygen into his system. Hurt lanced through Cade for his friend but the agony he felt for the torture Rafe had suffered through was like a gaping wound deep inside of him. He wanted nothing more than to pull Rafe into his arms but the man's rigid demeanor made it clear the last thing he wanted was anyone touching him.

Rafe suddenly went quiet and Cade could hear more than one person crying behind him. But Rafe only had eyes for his brothers.

"I've wasted twenty years of my life on you. No more," he muttered. "Not one more day," he said coldly and then turned and left.

Still stunned by Rafe's crushing admissions, it took Cade a moment to get moving and by the time he reached the sidewalk, Rafe had disappeared. His cell phone lay on the sidewalk and when Cade snatched it up, he saw that the tracking device was taped to the front of it.

CHAPTER 4

*R*afe slammed his laptop closed and shoved the offending computer away. Three days. Three days into his new beginning and he couldn't think for shit. Even the noise of the busy downtown street and the endless chatter of the people sitting around him in the café's patio seating area weren't helping him focus like they usually did. And all because he couldn't get the sight of Dom on his knees out of his head.

Chugging the rest of his coffee, Rafe grabbed his laptop and shoved it into his bag. He searched his wallet for an appropriate tip and tossed the cash on the small round table. Maybe it had been a mistake to come back to L.A. Maybe a fresh start meant starting over from scratch. He had enough cash stashed away in half a dozen offshore accounts that he could go anywhere he wanted. Hell, he didn't even need to work anymore and it wasn't like being a hacker was the most noble of professions. He could go legit – maybe volunteer his computer skills to a place that needed him. An image of Logan's crappy little foundation flashed in his mind and then the man himself was there as he wrapped his arms around his broken lover.

Jesus Fucking Christ! Rafe got up so fast he nearly knocked his chair over and several people looked at him curiously. He grabbed the chair and jammed it under the table, then left the patio area and began walking along the sidewalk that would take him the ten blocks back to his shitty hotel. That would be his second order of business after figuring out where to call home – he'd actually find a home. Moving from one run down hotel room to another every week was getting old.

"Rafe, get down!"

Rafe jerked at the sound of that familiar voice and a split second later something whizzed past his ear and suddenly the store window behind him shattered. Several screams penetrated the air as he instinctively hit the ground as a searing pain stabbed him in the upper left arm. Gunshots flew as people ran past him and then a big hand was closing around his right bicep and dragging him upwards.

"Move!" Cade shouted as he pushed Rafe around the corner and in between two buildings. Cade's grip on his arm was brutal as he shoved Rafe back against the wall and then stuck his head around the corner and began searching the perimeter, the gun in his hand at the ready.

"Let's go," Cade ordered roughly as he grabbed hold of Rafe again and led him to the end of the block and pushed him into a late model sedan. Cade climbed behind the wheel and calmly pulled the car away from the curb as several police cars raced past. He didn't acknowledge Rafe until they had gone a good ten blocks.

"How bad is it?" Cade asked as he glanced at where Rafe was putting pressure on the gash in his upper arm.

"Hurts like a motherfucker," Rafe bit out.

Cade pulled the car into a deserted parking lot and jammed it into park. Rafe flinched when Cade grabbed both edges of his shirt and ripped the sleeve open to expose the wound.

"Bullet grazed you," Cade murmured. He tore the rest of Rafe's sleeve off and balled it up and applied it to the injury. "Keep pressure on it." Cade put the car in gear and got back on road.

"What the hell is going on?"

Cade glared at him. "You tell me. You're the one who's got someone gunning for him."

Rafe felt his stomach drop out. "No," he said in confusion. "It was probably some random, freak thing."

"I saw the guy, Rafe. He was aiming at you and only you." Cade parked the car and Rafe looked up to realize they were at his hotel. "Key," Cade ordered as he held his hand out. Rafe winced as he used the hand on his injured arm to fish the room key out of his computer bag. "Stay behind me."

Rafe followed Cade to his room and stared in disbelief at the destruction before him. The few belongings he had were mostly clothes and those had been dumped on the floor and rifled through. But the rest of the room was ripped apart. The mattress was flipped and shredded on both sides like someone had cut into it. The drawers from the dresser lay broken on the floor and the table and nightstand were both overturned.

"What was he looking for, Rafe?" Cade asked coldly, his hard eyes pinning Rafe where he stood.

"I don't know," he responded. And it was the truth – he had no clue who had done this and why.

"Grab what you need and let's go," Cade said.

Rafe glanced at his meager possessions. What was the point? Everything he owned was replaceable. There were no sentimental photos or treasured knickknacks. He turned and left the room and got back into Cade's car. As the confusion over what was happening set in, he felt the panic start to rise.

"Rafe, look at me," Cade ordered, though his tone wasn't as harsh as it had been a minute ago. He forced himself to look at Cade and an overwhelming sense of relief swept through him which made no sense since this man was the last person he had ever wanted to see again aside from his brothers.

A rough palm settled around the back of his neck. "Everything's going to be okay," Cade said simply as he rubbed his thumb over the side of Rafe's throat before settling it on his pulse. The move shouldn't have eased Rafe's anxiety but it did. For the first time in his life when he'd needed to not be alone, he wasn't.

Rafe managed to nod and Cade finally released him and got the car moving. They drove for about thirty minutes before Cade pulled into a motel that was just as shabby as the last one. Rafe was too tired to care when Cade ordered him to stay put and the next thing he was aware of was Cade pushing him gently down into a hard chair. Fingers probed his injury and he let out a shout when Cade doused it with alcohol.

"Drink this," Cade said as he pushed a bottle into Rafe's hand.

"I don't drink," Rafe muttered as he tried to give the bottle back.

"You're going to need it," Cade replied as he opened a small pouch and began organizing the supplies within it.

"Cade, no," Rafe said as he saw Cade unwrap a needle.

"You need stitches and a hospital isn't really an option right now. Drink," he ordered again as he began preparing the thread.

"Have you ever done this before?" Rafe asked just before he took a long drag on the bottle of scotch. The alcohol burned and he immediately started gagging at the taste.

"Mostly on myself. Gonna hurt like a son of a bitch," he said mildly as he began rubbing a dark substance around Rafe's wound. Rafe forced down another drink and by the third he was starting to feel the heat spreading through his stomach. But he may as well have been drinking water because when the needle punctured his skin he felt it everywhere.

~

*C*ade turned off the bathroom light and went around to the side of the bed to drag the covers up over Rafe who'd fallen asleep within minutes of Cade helping him get settled on the cheap mattress. It was still light out but between the events of the last few days and the near miss this afternoon, Cade was spent. He stepped wearily out of his clothes and crawled under the covers next to Rafe and took a moment to study the man. He marveled at how young and at peace Rafe looked and he couldn't stop himself from reaching out to stroke his fingers over Rafe's cheek. Rafe flinched away and Cade automatically withdrew his hand but then to his surprise, Rafe shifted closer until his head was pressed against Cade's outstretched arm. The contact was minimal but electricity shot through him anyway. God, how he wanted this man.

Resisting the urge to draw Rafe closer to him, Cade leaned back so that he was staring at the ceiling and tried to get the image of that first bullet missing Rafe by just millimeters out of his head. If Rafe hadn't turned at the exact right moment when Cade called his name, it would all be over and he'd be telling the already devastated Barretti brothers that their little brother was gone for good.

The aftermath of the confrontation with Rafe at *Barretti's* had changed everything for Dom and Vin and the people that loved them. They were two of the strongest men Cade had ever known but Rafe's admission about what had happened to him had destroyed them and Cade knew that no matter what happened, Dom and Vin would never be able to forgive themselves.

He suspected that they'd both always held out hope that Rafe had had a decent life with his biological father because contemplating anything else would have made it impossible to function in the years after they lost him. But to know their baby brother's innocence had been brutally stolen within hours of him being ripped away was too much. And to hear how Rafe had waited for them to come save him had been the final blow.

Although he'd left shortly after Rafe to follow the man back to L.A., he'd kept in touch with Logan who had retreated with Dom to their house in the San Juan Islands. From the despair in Logan's voice he knew it was bad...really bad. A call to Mia had proven that Vin wasn't faring any better. And watching Rafe for the past three days had made it clear that as much as Rafe probably wanted to believe that he was moving on, the reality was that he wasn't. When the young man wasn't wandering aimlessly around the city, he was agitated and unfocused. He'd start working on his precious computer only to stop within minutes and slam it shut. Then he'd stare off into the distance for a while, shake himself loose from whatever dark thoughts had caused the pained look on his face and then he'd open the computer again and start typing away. And then the whole process would repeat itself.

Cade hadn't had a plan as to how to deal with the whole situation but the one thing he'd known from the moment Rafe had walked out of the restaurant, Cade couldn't just let him go. And it wasn't just his protective nature kicking in. No, there was something about Rafe that drew him in. Had him wanting more. More of what, he didn't really know. Just more.

Cade sucked in a breath when Rafe shifted again and pressed up against him. An arm reached across his chest and snaked around his side and he looked down, expecting to see Rafe awake. But he was still out. Desire rippled through Cade at the feel of the hard body pressed so closely to his. *This* – this was definitely what he wanted more of. Not just the mind blowing sex but the after part. This feeling of being connected to someone.

Cade let his arm drop down around Rafe's shoulders. Whatever 'this' was, it was temporary because he knew the second Rafe woke up he'd have a fight on his hands. Because as much as Rafe didn't want his brothers, he sure as hell needed them. Rafe Barretti was going home whether he liked it or not.

～

*R*afe noticed two things long before he opened his eyes. One - his arm hurt like hell. And two – the overwhelming heat beneath him. But since he wasn't struggling to breathe he knew the heat wasn't coming from him as the result of an impending panic attack.

When his whole upper body lifted slightly before falling back down, Rafe forced his eyes opened and confirmed what he had already suspected – that he was sprawled across Cade's chest, his hand tucked against Cade's armpit and a hard pillow of muscle beneath his head. One burly arm was wrapped around him like a band of steel and the other was stretched along his back, the broad palm splayed just above his ass. Thank God he still had his underwear on.

But unfortunately the thin fabric was doing little to protect him from the feel of one finger pressed against the top of his crack.

Another rise and fall of Cade's chest told Rafe the man was still asleep but with the way Cade was holding him, there was little chance he'd be able to extricate himself without waking him up. So sneaking off without a word was out. That meant he needed to ready himself for a fight because there was no way in hell he was spending another day with this man, would-be shooter be damned. If what Cade said was true and the guy really had been gunning for him – which seemed the likely scenario given the destruction to his motel room – then he'd get his ass on the first flight out of the country. Hacking and hiding – the two things he did best.

Rafe held his breath as Cade shifted slightly beneath him and he bit back a groan when the hand on his ass slid lower and cupped him. If he didn't know better he'd think the son of a bitch wrapped around him like a vine was awake but Cade's breathing never changed. His cock was aching as another shift had his lower half pressed against Cade's hip and he couldn't stop himself from humping against Cade in search of relief. But when the hand on his ass tightened even further he knew he'd been had.

"Asshole," he muttered as he tried to pull away from Cade.

Cade chuckled and then Rafe was flat on his back as Cade pressed his weight over him. "Morning to you too," Cade said softly and before Rafe could protest, those firm lips were closing over his. He tried to use his uninjured arm to push Cade back but instead he was wrapping it around Cade's shoulders, pulling him closer. His mouth betrayed him too because it instantly opened for Cade's seeking tongue and when Cade was the one to withdraw, his traitorous lips followed, refusing to release the other man. One more kiss, he told himself. One more and then he'd send Cade on his way.

∾

*C*ade sucked Rafe's tongue into his mouth and captured the other man's moan as Cade sank more of his weight down on him. He'd only meant to have a quick taste but was thrilled when Rafe had returned his kiss. He'd been hard all night from Rafe constantly shifting against him and waking up to the man practically humping his hip had been too much. And that ass. He knew copping a feel definitely wasn't going to win him any points but he'd done it anyway. It was tight and full and all he wanted to do was dip his fingers in between the perfectly round globes and explore. But the feel of slightly raised flesh was a reminder of the pain Rafe had endured and he wasn't about to push the other man into something he clearly didn't want.

And then Rafe had kissed him back. Had refused to release him, in fact.

Cade reached between their bodies and pushed Rafe's underwear down enough to free his engorged cock. When his hand closed around it, Rafe groaned and thrust up against him. It took only seconds for him to work his own dick free and then he held them together in his fist and began long, even strokes that had Rafe twisting beneath him desperately.

"Cade," Rafe murmured against his lips before he kissed him again.

Cade increased the pressure as well as the rhythm and let out a shout of pleasure as Rafe bit down on his shoulder when his orgasm hit him. The move triggered Cade's own release and he groaned as come splashed between their bodies.

"Fuck," Cade said as he released their cocks and leaned back enough so he could watch as he smeared his and Rafe's come together over Rafe's muscular abdomen. Rafe watched his hand intently, then dragged Cade's fingers to his mouth and licked them clean.

Cade would have given anything to spend the day pulling every ounce of pleasure out of their bodies as he could but he knew he was putting off the inevitable. He leaned down and gave Rafe a quick, hard kiss, ignoring the delicious taste of their release on the other man's tongue, and then sat up. "Go shower," he said gently as he pulled Rafe to a sitting position. "We'll talk after. Keep your bandage dry."

Rafe looked like he wanted to argue but Cade was glad when he didn't because Cade just wasn't ready for the fight he knew was coming.

∾

*R*afe sat on the edge of the bathtub and wrapped his arms around himself. His clothes along with a fresh shirt that he assumed was Cade's since the only one Rafe had left was torn and bloodied, were sitting neatly folded on the top of the toilet. He hadn't even heard Cade come in and put them there. And that simple, thoughtful act was fucking more with his head than the amazing things Cade had done to him in bed less than ten minutes ago. Common courtesy – that was all it was. A guy being nice.

He had no idea what the fuck to do with nice. Being disrespected, terrorized, brutalized – those things he could handle. But he had no clue how to deal with a man who reminded him not get his bandage wet and brought him his fucking clothes so he wouldn't have to go searching for them.

All he knew was that he wanted more and that scared the shit out of him.

∾

*C*ade had considered packing Rafe's stuff in the car while he was in the shower in the pathetic hope it would somehow speed up the battle they were about to go through, but not only did the guy not have enough shit to actually pack up, Cade didn't want to play the role of manipulative bastard. He would if it was the only way to get Rafe back to Seattle and the safety of his family, but he hated the thought of being yet another man that took Rafe's choices away.

He stiffened when Rafe came out of the bathroom and ignored the tug in his chest at the sight of Rafe's weary expression. Rafe closed the distance between them and reached for his bag. He kept his eyes lowered when he spoke.

"I don't want to see them," was all he said.

Cade knew exactly who 'them' was. "Okay."

Rafe nodded and stepped past him and headed for the car. The young man looked so worn out that Cade actually hesitated before going to the car himself. What if he was about to make things worse for everyone, especially Rafe?

CHAPTER 5

"*How* did you find me?" Rafe asked as he forced the breakfast sandwich down. Between the alcohol he'd consumed last night and the stunning turn of events that had him heading back to the city he swore he'd never set foot in again, he wasn't sure he'd be able to keep the greasy food down.

"I put a second tracker in your watch when you were in the shower the other night," Cade responded carefully.

Rafe glanced at the platinum watch on his wrist. It had cost him a small fortune but something about it had drawn him in when he'd seen it at the jewelry store he passed every day on one of his many coffee runs. Beautifully perfect precision with every gear and wheel aligned and balanced so that it was completely self-sufficient and always true. Cade had been smart to know he'd be unlikely to part with the watch as easily as he had his phone.

"They shouldn't have sent you after me," Rafe said quietly as he watched the scenery fly by.

"They didn't. They don't know I'm here."

Rafe glanced at Cade in confusion.

Cade kept his eyes on the road when he said, "I left Seattle an hour after you did."

"Why?" Rafe managed to ask though he wasn't sure he really wanted to know. But Cade didn't answer him. "You've been watching me all this time?" Still no answer.

"Pull over," Rafe said firmly. He was surprised when Cade did as he asked and turned on a side road and then parked at the entrance to an overgrown service road.

"Why, Cade?" Rafe demanded when Cade put the car in park and turned it off.

It took Cade a long time to answer. "I needed to make sure you were okay."

Rafe got out of the car and slammed the door shut and just started walking. He stepped over the chain preventing cars from going further down the service road. He didn't have to look back to know Cade was right behind him.

"I don't want your fucking pity!" he snapped as he lengthened his stride. Humiliation burned through him.

"It's not pity," Cade said evenly.

"Well whatever it is, I don't want it!"

"What do you want?" Cade asked gently. He didn't even sound winded while Rafe felt like his lungs were going to explode.

He finally stopped but didn't turn around. The truth hit him hard. "I want to go back."

～

*C*ade waited in silence as Rafe stared at the deserted dirt road in front of them. "I want go back to before I started all this. I want to have never met you…any of you," he said tiredly.

That stung but Cade couldn't blame him. "Why didn't you send the emails?" he asked.

It took Rafe a while to answer.

"I didn't like who I was becoming." Rafe turned slowly but refused to look directly at him. "I shouldn't have done that to you," he said quietly. "I shouldn't have left you there on the floor like that."

This hadn't really been the direction he wanted this conversation to go in. "Then why did you?" he heard himself ask, hoping like hell he managed to keep the hurt out of his voice.

Blue eyes finally lifted to meet his. "I needed to make sure you knew it wasn't more than it was."

"Just a quick fuck, right?" Cade said, his anger growing. "Don't worry, message received," he bit out and turned to head back to the car. "We need to get moving. It's a long drive." He thought he heard Rafe say his name but he was beyond caring.

Cade didn't wait to see if Rafe would follow. His head start gave him a few extra moments to collect himself as he got back in the car. The rest of the day was spent in silence as they worked their way north and Cade finally gave in to his exhaustion and found a hotel to stop at for the night just past the Oregon border. He picked something nicer and made sure to get two beds this time around since he sure as hell wasn't going to put himself through the torture of sharing a bed with a man who wanted nothing to do with him.

They had dinner at the diner that was part of the truck stop next to the hotel but Rafe was so jumpy that he barely touched his food. It wasn't until halfway through the meal that Cade realized being around the truckers and their rigs might be triggering horrendous memories for Rafe.

"Come on," he said as he tossed some money down on the table.

Cade unlocked their room and stepped aside to let Rafe in but didn't enter. He was too keyed up to be cooped up with Rafe just yet so he said, "Lock this – I'll be back in a second."

He didn't give Rafe a chance to answer before pulling the door shut. He heard it lock and then hurried to the gas station next door. He grabbed a few things for Rafe including a tooth brush and some snacks and dropped them on the counter. Before he could think better of it, he had the clerk get him a couple packs of cigarettes and he hurriedly unwrapped the first pack as he began walking back to the hotel. Logan would be pissed but he was too wound up to care. It was either this or drown himself in a bottle of liquor and since he needed to keep his wits about him, the latter wasn't an option.

He dropped down onto the step leading up to the hotel and fished a cigarette out. Just as he went to light it, his phone rang and he grimaced. He was glad to see it wasn't Logan calling him because then he would have felt like an even bigger shit for giving in to his bad habit.

"Hey asshole, how's life in Hicksville?" he muttered.

"Funny," his friend Jax said.

"Shouldn't you be fucking the hot vet right about now?" Cade drawled as he glanced at his watch.

"He got called to an emergency. Something about a goat expecting triplets."

"That's some new life you picked out for yourself."

Jax laughed. "It sure is," he said softly and Cade could hear the man absolutely meant it. Former FBI agent turned small town cop and hooking up with a single dad with a six-month old kid. He never would have guessed it in a million years but it sure as hell was working for the man he considered a brother.

"Where are you?" Jax asked.

Cade glanced around the parking lot. It was just too long of a story to tell so he just said, "On a job."

Jax was silent for a moment before he said, "Let me guess, it's complicated."

Cade laughed as the words he'd said to Jax were tossed back at him. Complicated didn't even begin to cover the shit storm going on inside of him. "Yeah," he finally responded to his friend.

"He worth it?" Jax asked softly.

He hesitated before finally saying, "Yeah." *Fuck.*

"Make it work, Cade," Jax responded. "Get past complicated and just make it work."

Cade heard the tell-tale sound of a baby crying in the background. "Go take care of your daughter, Jax. And tell the hot vet I said hi."

He disconnected the call and stuck his phone in his pocket. He glanced at the cigarette in his hand and sighed. Snatching up the two packs from the ground, he tossed them and the lighter into the garbage can at the end of the walkway before searching out the room key. One more night. He could get through one more night.

~

*F*our days. Four days and less than a dozen words had been spoken between them.

Rafe tried to focus on the screen in front of him. The sooner he figured out who he'd pissed off enough to come after him guns blazing, the sooner he could find a way to neutralize the threat and get out of this place. Not that being in Cade's apartment actually meant he was around Cade. No, the exact opposite was true. He could count on one hand how many times Cade had spoken to him in person since he'd shown Rafe the guest room. After that it had been a series of texts telling him to stay in the apartment as well as a warning not to remove the tracker from his watch.

Their last night in the hotel and the drive back to Seattle hadn't been any better. Cade had been sullen and withdrawn and Rafe hadn't even tried to draw him out. He didn't have the right after the shitty things he'd said to Cade about what he wanted – or rather didn't want – out of their relationship. Well, he'd gotten what he asked for. There was absolutely no fucking relationship.

But Cade was still doing the little acts of kindness that were driving Rafe insane with confusion and guilt. The man had instinctively known that he had been uncomfortable eating at the truck stop as truckers came and went and had given up finishing his own dinner so they could get out of there. And then he'd brought Rafe snacks and a toothbrush and other incidentals to get him through the night. The first morning after they'd arrived back at Cade's apartment, a bag full of new clothes had been looped over his bedroom door. When he'd tried to thank Cade before he left for the day, Cade had dismissed his gratitude and asked for his phone, replacing it with a new one, presumably in case his new enemy was tracking the old one.

After four days he was no closer to figuring out who was after him and he'd ruined any chance at a friendship with the one man who'd treated him decently since Gary had destroyed his life. It amazed him that it had taken being around Cade to realize how lonely Rafe really was.

Rafe heard the front door open and glanced at his watch. A thrill of excitement went through him at seeing it was barely four o'clock. If Cade was home for the night, maybe they could have some dinner, talk. He left the bedroom and hurried into the living room, ignoring the skittering of nerves along his spine. Jesus, was that a fucking smile spreading across his mouth?

As he rounded the couch he came to a dead stop at the sight of a huge Rottweiler sitting near the entryway to the kitchen. The dog cocked his head at him and then quickly jumped up and trotted over to him, a string of drool hanging off his massive jowls. He stiffened as the animal sniffed him.

"Baby," came a voice from the kitchen and then a young kid was peeking around the corner. "He won't hurt you none," the kid said to him as he came into the living room, a bag of chips in one hand, a soda in the other.

"I'm Eli," he said as he tucked the chips under his chin and reached out his hand.

"Rafe," Rafe responded and returned the surprisingly firm handshake.

Eli went to the living room and dropped down on the couch, then pulled open one of the doors on the walnut coffee table. "You like Call of Duty?" he asked as he pulled out a couple of video game controllers.

"Um, I've never played before," he admitted. His mind was racing as he realized who the kid was.

"Can't be much worse than Cade. He sucks," Eli said with a snort as he held out one of the controllers expectantly.

"He's not here," Rafe said as he went to sit on the couch.

"I know. He lets me hang out here on nights my mom has to work late. Even if he's not home," Eli said as he turned the 50-inch TV on.

Rafe leaned back and studied the controller in his hand as Eli started explaining how the game worked. He only half listened as he studied the boy. He guessed him to be in his early teens and he could almost be considered pretty with his slight frame, coal black hair and darker skin tone.

Less than a week ago he was arguing the merits of saving kids like Eli with Logan and now he was sitting next to him. Because his brother had done something – he'd stepped up when this kid needed someone.

"Got it?" Eli asked.

Rafe managed a nod though he really hadn't heard much of what Eli had said about the game. Within a minute of Eli starting up the game, Rafe was already dead and Eli was laughing so hard that his character met his doom a moment later. The kid gave him a goofy grin as he restarted the game and gave Rafe some tips on how to stay alive longer. An hour later and he was so invested in the animated carnage that he nearly yelled at Eli when he paused the game so they could take a bathroom break.

As he waited for Eli to return, the Rottweiler came up to him and nudged his hand. He didn't have much experience with dogs or any animals for that matter so he was surprised when the dog dropped his big head in his lap.

"I think that's why Mrs. Barretti named him Baby," Eli said as he trotted back into the living room and gave the dog a pat before settling down on the couch once more.

Rafe froze in the act of petting the animal. "This is Dom's dog?" he asked quietly, his heart catching when he said his brother's name.

"Used to be. Dom gave him to me. He said I could take better care of him but I think it's 'cause he knew Baby makes me feel better," Eli responded as he stuffed a handful of chips in his mouth.

"How does he make you feel better?" Rafe asked as Baby pressed against his hand and he resumed his petting.

"I don't know, I guess sometimes when I get scared Baby knows how to make it go away." Eli's voice dropped off and he could tell the kid was embarrassed.

"He's a great dog, Eli. I'm glad you have him," Rafe said.

Eli studied him for a moment. "If you want to borrow him sometime, that'd be okay I guess," Eli offered.

Rafe glanced up in surprise.

"If you get scared or something."

Understanding dawned as Eli nervously looked away and pretended to check something on his game controller.

"Were you at the restaurant that night, Eli?"

Eli nodded. Rafe remembered more than he wanted to about the night he'd blurted out his humiliating secret in front of his brothers and their friends but he hadn't really paid attention to all the people who were in attendance.

"Eli," he said gently and waited till the kid looked at him. "Thank you for the offer," he said as he looked down at Baby. "I'll let you know, okay?"

Eli nodded and a shy smile spread across his features. He grabbed Rafe's controller and handed it to him. "A few more games and you'll suck even less than Cade does."

"I heard that."

They both turned to hear the door close and Cade entered with a bag in his hands. His eyes held Rafe's for a brief moment but whatever flashed in them was gone before Rafe could ponder it for too long. His own pulse had notched up dramatically at the sight and sound of the other man.

Eli and Baby both ditched him to follow Cade into the kitchen and he listened as the kid rambled on about the day's events. All three came back into the living room a moment later and it wasn't until Eli sat on the opposite end of the couch and handed Cade a third controller that Rafe felt his heart go into overdrive. The only place for Cade to sit was between him and Eli and by Cade's hard look at the open space on the couch, he was none too happy about it. But he sat anyway, his thigh brushing Rafe's briefly and Rafe nearly moaned at the contact.

Cade's overwhelming presence proved to be too much of a distraction on his senses and his avatar paid the price as he was blown to bits over and over again. Another half an hour passed before Eli's phone rang and he paused the game to answer it.

"Yeah, be right down," Eli said. "Gotta go," he said as he tucked his controller back in the cabinet. "Later," he said to Cade as they bumped fists. "Bye, Rafe."

"Bye," Rafe said. Cade was up and moving away from him even before the door closed and Rafe immediately felt the loss. So much for hoping things would be different.

~

Cade unpacked the rest of the groceries he'd left in the bag after Eli had convinced him to play a couple of rounds of the kid's favorite video game. He hadn't wanted to be in such close proximity to Rafe and sitting next to him had been pure torture. Every time Rafe moved, Cade had felt it. Every sigh, every grunt of excitement, even the guy's amazing smell had Cade on edge from the moment he sat down. If Eli hadn't been there, he would have had Rafe splayed out along the supple leather in no time.

"He's a good kid," he heard from behind him.

"Yeah, he is," Cade said as he forced himself to focus on the task at hand.

"He said you let him come over when his mom has to work late."

He didn't need to turn to know that Rafe was just feet from him. "Yeah. They live in an okay neighborhood but I guess he feels safer here because it's more secure. It's been like that since he was abducted. I try to be here on the days I know he's coming over after school."

Rafe fell silent behind him but a quick glance over his shoulder showed that Rafe was leaning against the counter that separated the kitchen from the living room. It would only take two strides to reach him...

"I wouldn't have pegged you for a "kids" kind of guy."

"Yeah, well, there's a lot of things you have and haven't pegged me as, aren't there?" he said coldly. He jammed the last of the groceries into the cupboard and turned to leave the kitchen but Rafe stepped in his path.

"Cade, I didn't mean anything by that," Rafe said solemnly.

"Sure," Cade said as he stepped past Rafe, ignoring the surge of lust that went through him when their bodies touched. "I'm going to go for a run," he said quickly as he headed towards his room. It took just moments to change into sweats and a tank top and when he hurried towards the front door he saw that Rafe was still where he'd left him in the kitchen. Not his problem, he reminded himself as he left the apartment.

He'd wanted to make sure Rafe was safe and he'd done that – his building was as secure as they came. His place was also big enough so that he could easily avoid the other man as much as possible and he'd done an admirable job in the four days they'd been back in Seattle. The second Rafe figured out who was targeting him, Cade would take care of it and this would be over. No more second guessing himself about wanting someone who didn't want him. No more sleepless nights as he thought about the man in the next room, dreamed about his whipcord body and perfect mouth, raged about the torture and abuse that had been inflicted upon him. He had no idea if Gary Price was alive or dead but he knew the fucker would wish he were dead if Cade ever got his hands on him.

An hour of running did little to ease the tension in his system but since he knew it would likely take a coma to do that, he headed back to his apartment. Rafe wasn't in any of the common areas and his bedroom door was closed. It was a cowardly thing to do but Cade checked the tracking software on his phone to confirm Rafe, or at least his watch, were still in the apartment rather than knocking on his door to make sure he was there. But his heart nearly stopped when he opened his own door and saw Rafe sitting on his bed.

It took him a few seconds to recover before he said, "What is it? Did you need something?"

Rafe laughed but it sounded uneven and hollow. God, what he wouldn't give to hear Rafe laugh for real.

"Yeah, I need to know how to not always say the wrong thing around you."

Cade went to his dresser and put his phone down. He usually put it on the nightstand but he didn't trust himself to get that close to Rafe, especially seeing how vulnerable the other man looked.

"Don't worry about it," he said. "We're fine."

Another laugh. "I don't know much about you, Cade. But I do know you're not a liar so don't start now."

Frustration went through Cade. "What do you want, Rafe? You said you wanted to go back to before you met me. This is the best I can do," he said tiredly. "Find the fucker that wants you dead and I'll be out of your life for good."

Cade started to head to his bathroom but Rafe's words stopped him cold.

"I lied."

Cade didn't respond or turn around.

"I wish I hadn't started this whole thing with Dom and Vin but I wouldn't change meeting you."

He heard Rafe get up and come closer. A hand coasted down his back and then disappeared. But the effect was devastating on Cade's senses. He knew that all he had to do was turn around and he could have Rafe in his arms again, could feel their bodies perfectly aligned, could taste the lush mouth that fit his like it had been made for him.

He heard Rafe sigh before he said, "Could we at least try being friends? The kind that say hello to each other once in a while, maybe eat a meal together? Or did I fuck any chance of that up too?"

A better man would say yes. A better man would overlook the wounds this man had inflicted on him, however unintentional they may have been. A better man would set aside the fucked up emotions churning in his gut.

But he wasn't a better man so he simply said, "I don't need any more friends" and went into the bathroom, closing the door behind him before he could see what impact his words had.

CHAPTER 6

"How's he doing?" Cade asked as Logan led him to the kitchen.

"Not great," Logan admitted as he poured Cade a cup of coffee and settled on one of the stools surrounding the huge island in the modern kitchen. Normally Cade marveled at the sight of the water and mountains that made up the view of Dom and Logan's island house but today he had no interest beyond the man in front of him and the well-being of his best friend who had yet to make an appearance. Logan himself looked exhausted which meant Dom was probably ten times worse.

"And Vin?"

Logan just shook his head.

"Fuck," Cade whispered.

"We're going to head back to the city next week. Try to get back into the swing of things again."

Cade nodded. "There's something I need to tell you. Both of you," he said quietly. "But it may make things worse."

"They can't get much worse," Logan responded.

They both heard footsteps and Cade actually felt like someone had punched him in the gut when he saw Dom enter the kitchen. The man looked like he'd aged a decade. His skin was pale and drawn tight, his eyes sunken and hollow. He'd definitely lost weight and his normally bald head was covered with a week's worth of growth. The only positive thing was when Dom wrapped his arm around Logan and placed a kiss on his neck before he turned his attention to Cade.

"Hey."

"How you doing, Dom?"

Dom just shrugged and sank down on the stool next to Logan.

"Can I make you something to eat?" Logan asked as he settled a hand over Dom's.

"Not hungry," Dom replied as he shook his head.

Logan twined his fingers with Dom's and waited until his lover finally looked at him. "You need to eat, Dom," Logan whispered. "Please."

Dom finally nodded and pulled Logan's hand up to his mouth and brushed a brief kiss over it.

Logan jumped up and started pulling things out of the fridge. Cade knew it was important to get food into Dom's system so he held off on any talk of Rafe until after Dom had forced down half the sandwich. He managed to keep the topic of conversation on the things going on at the office but when Dom pushed his plate away, Cade knew it was time.

"I have some news on Rafe," he said.

Pain lanced across Dom's features. "Is he okay?"

Fuck, this was going to be bad.

"He's fine. He's back in Seattle. At my place," he added.

Confusion went across both Logan and Dom's features but before they could jump to their own conclusions, he spit out the rest.

"I followed him to L.A. to make sure he was okay. Someone took a shot at him."

Dom stood so quickly the stool fell over.

"He's safe, Dom. The bullet grazed him but he's okay. He's holed up at my apartment."

"Who?" Dom managed to spit out.

"He's not sure. It probably has to do with someone he's hacked in the past. He's looking through his files and I've got Desi seeing what she can find out."

"Oh, God," Dom said in an agonized voice. He began pacing the room and then suddenly lashed out at several items sitting on a small side table. "Son of a bitch!" he screamed as he threw the table over. Logan watched in pained silence but didn't intervene.

"I swear to God, I'm going to find that fucking monster and tear him apart," Dom snarled as the contents of the sideboard went flying next. Cade had no doubt that Dom was talking about Gary Price. A couple more items hit the ground before Dom quieted. At that point Logan got up and went to Dom and wrapped his arms around him. Even from where he sat, Cade could see Dom grab Logan in a painful looking hold but the younger man didn't object. In fact, Cade could hear him murmuring in Dom's ear and then Dom was nodding. Cade felt like an intruder on the intimate moment and used the time to clear the few dishes from the island. By the time he turned around, Dom had eased his hold on Logan and he shifted so that his eyes could connect with Cade's.

"Can I see him?" Dom whispered.

It was completely fucked up that Dom had to ask him for permission to see his own brother and answering Dom was one of the hardest things he would ever have to do.

"He's not ready, Dom."

Dom closed his eyes as he nodded.

"He'll get there. He just needs a little bit of time," Cade offered, though he wasn't really sure that was true. Maybe if he hadn't pushed Rafe away last night, he could have figured out where Rafe was at with talking to his family.

"Keep him safe, Cade," Dom said softly just before he dropped a kiss on Logan's lips and left the room.

"I'm sorry, Logan," Cade said but Logan raised his hand and shook his head.

"He needed to know. We both did."

"You want me to tell Vin?" Cade asked.

"No, I'll tell him. He and Mia were thinking about coming up here for the weekend. Try and get away from things for a while."

Cade nodded. "I'll keep you posted," he said as he stood. He wasn't surprised when Logan hugged him before showing him out. The confrontation had physically and mentally exhausted him and he wished like hell he wouldn't have to relive it or the shit that had happened with Rafe last night over and over on the long drive back to the city.

~

"*T*hanks again," Rafe said as he waved once more to the woman before opening the door. "I should have something for you by Monday."

"What the fuck are you doing?" came a heavy voice as a burly hand closed around his arm.

Seeing an enraged Cade wasn't a surprise – the surprise had been in how long it had taken for Cade to come and get him. He'd had nearly a half an hour to sit with Logan's Assistant Director, Constance. The woman had talked his ear off the whole time and he'd met more people than he could even remember, but he'd actually found himself enjoying learning more about the foundation's goals and milestones.

"What the hell are you doing here?" Cade snapped as he glanced at the door behind him. Rafe was about to respond when Cade suddenly dragged him to his car and shoved him into the passenger seat.

The entire car shifted when Cade dropped down into the driver's seat and the tires actually squealed when Cade pulled the car away from the curb.

"Haven't you done enough?" Cade snapped. "You've destroyed both your brothers! Dom's a fucking zombie and Vin won't speak to anyone but Mia! What more do you want?" he snarled. "You gonna track Ren down too and fuck him up even more than he already is?"

Cade's rage was palpable and Rafe was actually afraid to respond.

Cade had never been abusive with him but the level of fury that was coursing through the man had him second guessing that now.

"Cade," he began.

"Shut the fuck up, Rafe!"

God, how many times had he heard that in his life before? The 'Rafe' part was always replaced with 'Boy' but the tone was exactly the same. As he felt his pulse start to increase and the tell-tale pain in his chest, he closed his eyes and tried to focus on the numbers and letters running across the imaginary computer screen in his head. But it was all gibberish and his panic went up another notch.

"Shit," he heard from what seemed like far away which didn't make any sense because the rocking back and forth motion of his body proved he was still in the car.

"Rafe, look at me. Rafe, please, I'm sorry."

He felt heat on his neck but cold everywhere else.

"Breathe in, baby. Real slow."

God, he loved that voice. It was so easy to focus on and so he did. After several long, agonizing minutes, the pain in his chest began to ease and each breath came easier and easier. When he finally opened his eyes, he realized they were in fact still in the car and the air conditioning was going full blast. The heat he still felt was coming from Cade's fingers rubbing circles along the back of his neck as well as their foreheads being pressed together.

"I'm sorry," Cade whispered over and over.

"I'm okay," Rafe said as he closed his hand over Cade's arm. "I'm okay," he said again and he felt Cade nod against him before finally pulling back and releasing him.

Cade got out of the car and Rafe realized they were in the garage of Cade's building. He got out and followed Cade to the elevator and as they waited for the car to come down to their level, he watched Cade shift in agitation. His anger had faded but he was still keyed up.

"Cade," he started to say but Cade held out his hand and shook his head.

Rafe fell silent and as soon as they got in the elevator he pressed himself into the corner and kept his mouth shut. But the second the doors closed, Cade grabbed his arm and yanked him forward.

"I don't want to be your God damn friend," Cade bit out just before he crushed his mouth over Rafe's and automatically sought entry. The second he opened his lips, Cade's tongue was stroking over his and he groaned when Cade pushed him back against the cool metal of the elevator wall. Hands immediately grabbed his ass and a thick thigh pressed between his legs. He was instantly hard and he began rubbing his pelvis over Cade's thigh in desperation.

He didn't even know the elevator had opened until Cade grabbed his hand and dragged him down the short hallway to his apartment. Cade's mouth was on his again the second he entered the code for the door and he was quickly maneuvered into the apartment. But they didn't make it far because Cade shoved him against the door and kissed him again as he began working his own shirt off.

Rafe dropped his head back against the door as Cade clutched him by the neck and held him still so he could kiss his way down his throat. Teeth nipped at him as a hand stroked under his shirt and over his abdomen. He reached down and grabbed the hem of his shirt and dragged it up over his head. The open invitation had Cade licking and kissing his way down his chest but when he reached for Rafe's jeans, Rafe snagged his wrist. He gently pushed Cade back a few steps until his back hit the opposite wall and then he dropped to his knees.

"Rafe, you don't have to," Cade said hoarsely as Rafe stroked his hands over Cade's slacks, his fingers closing over the steely length beneath the smooth fabric.

"I know," Rafe whispered as he worked the button and zipper free and the pants slid to the floor. The underwear quickly followed.

"Rafe," Cade said softly and he looked up to see Cade studying him earnestly. Something went through him at Cade's look of concern. He cared more about Rafe being okay with what was about to happen then getting Rafe's mouth on him.

Any hesitation he had disappeared and he leaned in to run his tongue over the flared head. The salty flavor had him quickly sucking the tip in his mouth so he could run his tongue lovingly over the slit and then around the ridge beneath the head.

Fingers sifted gently through his hair and he glanced up to watch Cade watching him. He was stunned when Cade carefully pulled free of his mouth and then leaned down to kiss him. Their tongues danced sweetly over each other for several long seconds before Cade drew back. Rafe grabbed Cade's hips and held him still as he sucked Cade's dick back into his mouth, the wide girth stretching his mouth. As he pulled Cade deeper down his throat on every stroke, he felt no urgency from the man above him, just soft, almost reverent petting on his head. No grabbing of his hair or neck, no slamming forward until he gagged.

Rafe relaxed his throat as Cade's length slid all the way in and his nose was pressed against the rough hair of Cade's groin. He drew back slowly, swirling his tongue as he went and then grazed his teeth gently over the crown before sucking him in again. Cade groaned above him. Rafe let his hands reach around to cup Cade's ass and a memory of the tight flesh flexing beneath his palms as he drove into Cade assailed him. He swallowed around Cade's dick and Cade let out a loud curse. He felt a warm palm settle on his upper back and then Cade was leaning over him, his broad hands massaging their way down his back as Rafe continued his long, torturous pulls.

"So beautiful," Cade whispered above him as he finally straightened so he could watch Rafe and the lust along with some other unidentifiable emotion in Cade's eyes had Rafe sucking on him hard and dragging his hips forward. Cade seemed to get the message and began to gently thrust into his mouth. Rafe let his hands search out the two heavy sacks and he rolled them between his fingers as he hollowed out his cheeks and intensified the suction as Cade slid in and out of him.

He knew Cade was still holding back so Rafe slid a finger between Cade's cheeks and sought out his pulsing hole.

"Fuck," Cade shouted as Rafe brushed it, then dipped the tip of his finger inside. Cade's fingers tightened in his hair but he felt no fear and he eagerly opened his mouth wider as Cade began to earnestly fuck him.

"I'm gonna come," Cade warned and Rafe knew he was going to pull out so he grabbed the man's ass once more and pulled his hips forward and held them there as Rafe sucked as hard as he could. As the first shot of semen hit the back of his throat, he moaned and closed his eyes in pleasure. He barely registered Cade's shout as more liquid fire spilled down his throat and he swallowed hungrily every time Cade punched forward. Long after the last drop fell on his tongue, Rafe continued to bathe Cade's cock with attention and when he finally released it, Cade was there to drag him to his feet for a soul wrenching kiss.

"I want you inside me," Cade whispered against his lips and then he was being dragged to Cade's bedroom. Cade made love to his mouth as his nimble fingers removed the rest of Rafe's clothes and then a fist closed around his hardness. He was so sensitive that he cried out at the contact and when Cade pushed him back on the bed and closed his mouth over his cock, Rafe moaned and threw his arm over his eyes. If he saw Cade sucking him, he knew it would end him before he had the chance to be buried deep inside the other man's body and he wasn't giving up that opportunity for anything.

Cade must have sensed how close he was because Rafe felt him pull off and then a condom was being rolled down his length. Lube followed and then Cade was drawing him up and off the bed. Cade bent over the edge of the bed and pulled back one cheek to expose his hole – the one already slick with lube. Rafe reached out and ran his fingers over the quivering, pulsing opening and he slid one finger in.

"More," Cade let out on a groan.

Rafe added another finger. He twisted his wrist and curved his fingers and suddenly Cade shouted and pushed back on him hard. "Yes, fuck," Cade said.

Rafe realized he must have hit Cade's prostate and he quickly did it again. With each pass Cade was moaning and desperately twisting against Rafe's fingers. Rafe reached around Cade's hips and felt Cade's erection brush his hand.

"Rafe, please," Cade groaned as he glanced over his shoulder at Rafe.

Rafe pulled his fingers out and ran his hands over Cade's perfect skin. It wasn't enough, he realized. It wasn't enough.

"Turn over," he said softly. "I need to see you."

～

*C*ade's heart tightened in his chest at Rafe's words and he was so caught off guard by the request that it took Rafe's gentle hands rolling him to his back to get him moving. Rafe urged him further back on the bed so he was in the middle of it. When Rafe climbed over his body and leaned down to kiss him, he opened his legs to make room for him and groaned when Rafe's tongue licked over his. The raw, clawing need inside of him turned into a slow building burn as Rafe showered him with soft, sweet kisses.

Jesus, was this what making love was? He was getting as much pleasure, if not more, from the feel of Rafe's body sinking down onto him as fingers explored every muscle and curved over every surface. Heat flooded his system and his nerves lit up as Rafe worshiped him and by the time Rafe kissed and touched his way down to Cade's lower body, Cade was writhing in blind need. Fingers probed him gently once more and then Rafe's cock began to breach him. His body opened willingly to Rafe and the man slid in easily until the wiry hair at his base brushed against Cade's flushed skin. And then Rafe was back over him, their slick bodies aligned once more as Rafe began to gently thrust into him.

Rafe's strokes were slow and deep as he continued to trail kisses all over Cade's face and mouth. He wanted to tell Rafe it was too much but he couldn't speak because the pleasure was consuming him, driving him higher. Arms disappeared under his back and curled up over his shoulders as Rafe finally began to increase the pace and Cade moaned every time Rafe slid into him as far as he could go. Cade's eyes drifted closed when a hand snaked between their bodies and began stroking him but he was drawn so tight with arousal that he couldn't move, couldn't think beyond the feel of Rafe's skin on his, his mouth pressed into the curve of his shoulder, his shaft driving him higher and higher, every peak greater than the last.

His orgasm hit him without any warning at all and he reached down to grab Rafe's ass to hold him inside of his body as Rafe shouted against his neck. The muscles beneath his palms clenched over and over as Rafe emptied himself inside of Cade and he wished like hell there wasn't a latex barrier separating them. His body continued to spasm as Rafe jerked inside him and then Rafe's mouth was searching his out again. He had no idea how long they kissed for but when Rafe finally slipped free of him, fear shot through Cade and he tightened his grip on the hard body still covering his.

"I'm not going anywhere," Rafe whispered against his lips before placing one last kiss on his mouth and then dropping his head to Cade's chest. An hour or four could have passed for all he knew when Rafe finally disentangled himself from Cade's arms and rose from the bed. Disappointment went through him and he turned on his side so he wouldn't have to watch the man walk away from him yet again. But a moment later, strong hands were gently turning him on his back and Rafe began cleaning him with a warm washcloth. Cade couldn't remember having such an intimate moment like this with anyone and he was ashamed he'd never taken the time to do this to any of the lovers he'd so callously fucked and then dismissed.

Rafe tossed the washcloth on the nightstand and leaned over Cade. "Can I stay here tonight?" he asked as he brushed his fingers over Cade's cheek.

Cade couldn't manage any words so he just nodded. When they were settled under the covers, Rafe ended up pressed against his chest but he wasn't sure if he'd put him there or Rafe had positioned himself that way. Truth was he didn't fucking care, as long as he stayed that way. But as much as he wanted to stay in this quiet, peaceful moment, there was too much between them that they needed to clear up.

"What were you doing at Logan's foundation today?" he asked carefully.

Rafe's fingers coasted over his chest. "I wanted to see if they needed help with their computers or networking."

"You went there to volunteer?" Cade said in surprise. Rafe nodded against him.

"I said some pretty shitty things to Logan about what he was trying to accomplish," Rafe admitted. "Meeting Eli yesterday made me realize I was wrong. Saving even one kid…" he said softly, his voice dropping off.

"Logan wasn't there which was probably a good thing so I talked to his Assistant Director. She asked if I would take a look at their website. It's something I can do from here."

"You shouldn't have left," Cade muttered as he skimmed his hand down Rafe's back. His fingers caught on scar after scar.

Rafe turned his head so their gazes met. "I know. I was pretty upset and just needed to get out of here for a while," he offered. "It was stupid," he said softly.

They were both silent for a moment and then Rafe said, "It was a whip."

Cade's hand stilled as he realized he'd been absent-mindedly rubbing his finger over one of the scars on Rafe's back.

"You don't have to tell me," Cade said gently as he resumed stroking up and down's Rafe's entire back. Rafe turned his head away and Cade thought that was it but then he spoke softly, his words difficult to hear.

"It had some kind of metal prongs at the end though I didn't know that until after."

"After?" Cade prodded.

"After I agreed to it," Rafe said.

Cade forced himself not to react and kept up his even rhythm of trying to soothe Rafe with his light touch.

"He was Gary's dealer and one of my regulars. He offered me a lot of money to tie me up. He said it wouldn't really hurt and that I'd end up liking it. I asked him for a trade instead."

"Trade for what?"

"I asked him to make sure the next batch of heroin he sold to Gary was the really good stuff but not to tell Gary."

Cade's hand froze as he realized what Rafe was admitting to. "You wanted Gary to OD."

"He did," Rafe said, his voice hollow now. "One hit and I was free. He never even got the needle out of his arm."

"And these?" Cade whispered as he stroked over the scars once more.

Rafe laughed coldly. "I guess I should be glad the guy tied me up and ignored the safe word he told me to use or the whole thing would have been off after the first hit."

"Zip ties?" Cade said, his throat clogging with pain.

"They have no give," Rafe stated simply. "My hands were tied together above my head and when he flipped me from my back to my front they twisted so tight I was afraid the blood supply would be cut off. I begged him to untie me but I think he liked it when I did that. I lost count after the first dozen hits but I could feel the blood running down my back. By the time he was done fucking me he was covered in it but he seemed to like that too."

Cade felt like he was going to vomit and he tried to drag in some air to calm the nausea that burned his gut. Rafe didn't seem to notice his distress because he continued to speak with little emotion.

"He kept up his end of the bargain, though. Two days later, Gary was dead."

"How old were you?" Cade asked, fearing the answer.

"Fourteen."

Jesus.

"What did you do then?" Cade asked.

Rafe turned once again to look at him. "The same thing I'd been doing. Taking my customers' money and using their weaknesses against them."

"What do you mean?"

Rafe turned away again. "I learned pretty early on that the men were going to take what they wanted whether I fought them or not. So I figured out what role they wanted me to play and I played it and I started asking for things in return. Extra money that Gary didn't know about, a new pair of boots or a jacket for the winter. If a guy wanted me to be sweet, I was sweet. If a guy wanted me to call him Daddy I did it and then I'd ask him for a reward for being his good little boy. There was a teacher that brought me books. A computer guy gave me an old laptop. The manager of a motel let me live for free in one of the rooms for a daily blowjob and the occasional fuck. By the time I was sixteen I had enough money to get my GED and take some college courses on computers."

Rafe turned his whole body this time and Cade let his hand rest on Rafe's hip.

"I'm not a victim anymore so don't fucking feel sorry for me," he said firmly. "And I'm not going to apologize for any of it."

Cade knew Rafe was testing him. He closed his hands around Rafe's upper arms and pulled him further up his chest until their lips were millimeters apart.

"You don't owe me or anyone else an apology," he said softly. "And you were never a victim, Rafe. You were a survivor."

~

$\mathcal{R}$afe felt the knot of tension inside his stomach release as Cade kissed him. He'd thrown all his shit at Cade without any kind of filter and instead of pushing him away like he'd thought he'd do, Cade was literally pulling him in closer. Not being able to accurately predict Cade's responses scared the shit out of him but his only option was to keep pushing Cade away. And he was done with that. He had no idea what any of this meant in terms of their relationship or if they even had one. But he was done worrying about that too because he wanted whatever Cade was offering. If that was just mind blowing sex he'd absolutely take it. If it was more, he'd deal with that. He'd take whatever Cade was willing to give him and store the memory of being with this incredible man away in his mind so he could relive these moments when the shit in his head began to pile up.

"Come take a shower with me," Cade said between kisses. Rafe nodded, though in truth he wasn't ready to leave the safety of Cade's bed. His ugly reality didn't exist in Cade's arms. He wasn't a one-time prostitute who'd used his body to get what he needed and he wasn't a man willing to ruin innocent lives to seek revenge against the brothers he'd idolized. And he wasn't nameless when Cade held him.

But the shower turned out to be an extension of Cade's bed as Cade continued to lavish him with gentle touches and deep kisses. And when Cade used his mouth to drag yet another orgasm out of Rafe's drained body, he felt another wall come crashing down.

"Stay in here a while longer," Cade murmured against his lips. "I'll go fix us something to eat."

Even with the hot water raining down on him, the loss of Cade's body left him cold so he didn't linger. He went back to his room to grab some sweats and a T-shirt and then went to the kitchen where Cade was in the process of frying something in a pan.

"Can I help?" Rafe asked, hoping like hell things between them weren't going to be awkward.

"You mind peeling the tomatoes?" Cade asked as he pointed at the large bowl of tomatoes sitting in an ice bath. Rafe stilled at the sight.

"What are you making?" he asked.

"Spaghetti and meatballs. Homemade sauce," Cade said with a proud grin. He finally seemed to notice Rafe's sudden quietness.

"What?" Cade asked as he lowered the burner to its lowest setting.

"You put the tomatoes in an ice bath."

"Yes, after I boiled them. It makes them easier to peel. I learned it from…" Cade's voice suddenly dropped off.

"Dom?" Rafe supplied.

"Yeah. He taught me a few things so I wouldn't eat so much takeout."

"We used to help our mom cook sometimes. I watched mostly." A pang of loss went through Rafe. But it wasn't just for his mother. It was for the brother who'd showered him with praise even when he messed up the simplest tasks he'd been assigned.

"Rafe…"

"No, it's good. I actually know how to do this," Rafe said as he pulled the tomatoes out and put them on a cutting board. He gave Cade a reassuring smile and the other man finally went back to cooking the meatballs.

"Didn't your mom teach you how to cook?" Rafe asked as he worked.

Cade chuckled. "No. My mom was old school. A kitchen was the woman's domain. I guess that was actually more my dad's way of thinking and my mom just followed along. I suppose if she had any problem with it, she let God know because she was at church the rest of the time."

"And your dad?"

"A real man's man," Cade huffed. "Big believer in 'spare the rod, spoil the child'. Worked as a miner when I was little but fucked up his back and went on disability. Funny how it never kept him from coming after me with his belt though."

Rafe glanced up at Cade in concern. The words were spoken with casualness but the tone said a hell of a lot more. Cade must have felt his gaze because he sent him a quick look.

"Don't worry, as soon as I was big enough to hit him back, I did. He never laid a hand on me after that, especially since I outweighed him by fifty pounds by the time I was sixteen."

"There was no one else?" Rafe asked.

Cade shook his head.

"Do you still keep in touch with them?"

"No. I left home the day my father walked in on me fucking the football team's quarterback. My dad started ranting and raving about fags and sin and the devil," Cade said with a laugh.

"I told him to get the fuck out and then I finished reaming the quarterback before I packed up my stuff and left. My mom was reciting some bible shit as I walked out and kept begging me to repent so I wouldn't go to hell. No clue if they're alive or dead."

"Where'd you go when you left?"

Cade shrugged and was quiet so long Rafe was sure he wasn't going to answer.

"Cade," he said quietly. Cade stopped what he was doing and

turned to look at him and Rafe was surprised to see shame in Cade's eyes.

"You can tell me anything," Rafe said firmly. Cade studied him for a long beat and then finally spoke.

"I wasn't exactly a model citizen after that. I ended up hanging out with a group of guys whose main goal in life was to get wasted, snort or shoot whatever shit they could get their hands on and fuck any woman who didn't care enough about herself to realize she could do better. And when they needed money they had no qualms about taking it." Cade's voice dropped off for a moment.

"I actually thought of them as my family," he added bitterly. "So what if we stole a couple of cars or convinced some shop owner that he should pay us money to "protect" his business? I convinced myself we weren't really hurting anyone."

Rafe managed to keep the surprise off his face. It was a side of Cade he never would have expected. And since Cade hadn't looked at him even once during his story, he was guessing it was something the other man didn't talk about often.

"One day my buddy decides we should jack this old lady as she's coming out of the bank. He tells her to hand over the keys to her car and her purse which she does. Then the fucker decides he wants her wedding ring. The thing probably wasn't worth more than fifty bucks but she starts crying and saying how it was all she had left of her husband. I tell the guy to leave it – that we should get out of there, but he goes nuts and decks her."

Before he realized what he was doing, Rafe was closing the distance between them and putting his hand over Cade's which was fisted around the handle of a knife he'd been using to cut vegetables. He was relieved when Cade released the knife, but concerned when the man still refused to look at him.

"She broke her hip when she fell but the son of a bitch kept railing at her to give him the ring. I laid him out with one punch," he muttered. "I stayed with the lady till the ambulance and the cops came. I hadn't turned eighteen yet so the judge gave me a choice –

prison time or join the army. Pretty easy choice," he said with a soft chuckle.

His eyes finally met Rafe's. "That lady showed up in court in a fucking wheelchair to ask the judge to go easy on me. Said I reminded her of her grandson who'd died the year before in a car accident. She told me to go do something good with my life."

Rafe smiled at the soft look that came over Cade's features.

"Two weeks later I had my GED and was on my way to Basic Training at Fort Benning."

Cade's body seemed to finally relax and he leaned over and brushed a quick kiss across Rafe's lips before he picked up the knife and got back to cutting vegetables.

"Joining the army was the best thing that ever happened to me because I met some guys who would become more of a family then my parents had ever been."

"Dom?" Rafe forced himself to ask, not sure if he really wanted to hear about his brother. He forced himself to break contact with Cade and return to his spot at the counter so he could finish the tomatoes.

Cade nodded. "Him and a couple of brothers – twins – that I met on my second tour. Ben and Jax. They had the perfect nuclear family – mom, dad, baby sister. They invited me to spend a lot of the holidays with them between deployments. Ben died a couple of years ago but I keep in touch with Jax. He moved to Montana a while back."

"And Dom?" Rafe heard himself ask.

"We were both deployed to Iraq after the Twin Towers were attacked. We hung out a bit but it wasn't until I finished my third tour that we reconnected. I was doing mercenary work at the time and I spent a lot of my time between jobs out here. When my last job went bad, he offered me work and I took it. Been here ever since."

"What happened at your last job?"

Cade's expression darkened. "A guy who hired us to rescue his daughter from the drug lord who'd abducted her failed to mention the guy was her boyfriend and she'd gone willingly. Or that she was enjoying playing Mrs. Drug Lord and had even learned to run the sex trafficking operation the guy was getting off the ground. Long story short, my team was okay with leaving the half dozen girls there to rot and save the bitch so they'd get paid. I disagreed and when the woman threatened to shoot a twelve-year-old girl in the head, I took her out. Needless to say the client wasn't real happy and my employer and I decided to part ways," Cade said dryly.

Cade began putting ingredients into a stock pot and took the peeled tomatoes from Rafe.

"So you started working for Dom?"

Cade nodded. "Mostly protection work. Dom runs the information security side of things while Vin works the personal protection and security side."

"And they sent you after me?" Rafe ventured as he pulled out a kitchen stool and sat, enjoying the sight of Cade in just a pair of jeans as he worked.

A smile skated over Cade's lips. "They found the bait you left them," Cade said with a smirk as he sent Rafe a mock accusatory look. "The IP address that you "forgot" to remove that just happened to lead us right to your fake office." Rafe blushed slightly.

"They sent me to check it out but I knew there was no way the hot guy I'd been trailing was the genius hacker." Cade set the pot to simmer and came over and placed his hands on the counter behind Rafe, in effect trapping him.

"I thought you were way too boring with your endless coffee runs and that fucking newspaper," Cade murmured just before he placed a soft kiss on Rafe's lips. "But I was so fucking turned on," Cade said before giving him another kiss. "And when you gave me that card…"

Rafe moaned as Cade's tongue pressed between his lips. The kiss didn't last long enough as far as Rafe was concerned.

"I wanted to rip that kid apart when I saw him touching you."

Rafe was surprised by the venom in Cade's tone. "That was the first night I'd met him," Rafe admitted. "I'd never been to that club either. It cost me a fortune to get in for just the night."

He felt Cade's hand close around the back of his neck and gently rub over it. He felt raw and exposed but for some reason he couldn't keep his mouth shut. "I hadn't been with anyone after my last trick. I tried once with a guy I was attracted to but I couldn't go through with it. I couldn't stand it when he touched me." He hesitated before finally saying, "You're the first guy I've ever…"

"Fucked?" Cade said softly.

Rafe nodded.

Cade kissed him. "You're the second guy I've given it up to but the first to make it absolutely perfect," he whispered before he kissed him again. Rafe lost track of time after that and would have been happy to forgo food for Cade's mouth but then his stomach growled and Cade drew back. One more brief kiss and Cade was releasing him and stepping back to the stove.

Thirty minutes later had Rafe literally licking the last of the sauce from his plate as he sat next to Cade on the living room couch.

"Good?" Cade asked with a laugh as he finished the last of his food.

Rafe nodded and licked around his mouth. The move had Cade staring hungrily at his lips. He wasn't sure which of them moved first but Rafe ended up on his back, the smooth leather dipping beneath him as Cade covered him with his body. He heard something clang and realized his plate had hit the floor but Cade didn't seem to give a shit because he was already dragging Rafe's shirt up and off his head. His sweats were dragged down just far enough to release his cock and he managed to fumble between his and Cade's body to get Cade's jeans loose enough to push off his ass.

Rafe stroked over the perfect mounds of flesh as Cade reached between their bodies and began rubbing their cocks together. Grunts and moans broke the silence as Cade mercilessly tortured them both with quick, hard tugs. Cade went over first giving Rafe a chance to see the look in his eyes as he was consumed by pleasure. It was enough for Rafe's body to give up the fight and he shouted and dug his fingers into Cade's ass as Cade humped over him. Firm lips licked over his neck and shoulder and Rafe couldn't help but wonder what it would have been like if Cade had been inside him. The thought scared the hell out of him but there was something else too – a quiver of need so strong he felt his whole body tense up again.

"You okay?" Cade asked.

Shit, was the man so in tune with him that he had sensed that Rafe was struggling with something? And if he cared enough to ask about even such a small thing, would he show the same care as he showed Rafe what the feel of a man deep inside of him was really supposed to be like?

Rafe managed a nod but nothing else as he finally eased his grip on Cade's ass.

"Let's go to bed," Cade murmured as he pulled Rafe to his feet. As they went towards the hallway where the bedrooms were, Rafe wanted to cry in relief when Cade bypassed the guest room and pulled him into his own bedroom.

CHAPTER 7

*C*ade felt instant panic when he reached out to the spot next to
him and felt only the coolness of the sheets.

"I'm right here," he heard Rafe say and he turned to see Rafe sitting
in an armchair in the corner of the room.

Relief went through Cade and he flopped back on the bed.

"I made coffee," Rafe said as he grabbed both cups sitting next to
him on the side table and went to the bed and sat on the edge of it, his
hip brushing Cade's waist. "Black, right?"

Cade leaned up against the headboard and nodded as he took
the cup.

"Can I ask you something?" Rafe said. At Cade's nod, Rafe continued. "You said something about Dom and Vin yesterday. You said I
destroyed them."

"Rafe," Cade began. "I was angry and scared when I discovered
you'd left the apartment. I shouldn't have said those things."

"Did you see them?" Rafe asked, his voice uneven.

Cade put the coffee down. "Just Dom. I haven't seen Vin. I've only
talked to Mia."

"It's bad?" Rafe asked and Cade flinched when he saw the man's
eyes brighten with what he suspected were tears.

As much as he would have liked to lie to Rafe, he knew he couldn't so he just nodded.

"And Ren?"

"He left a few weeks after Vin brought him home. He said he needed some time and he's been off the grid ever since."

Rafe nodded and turned his head away. "I didn't mean to say so much in the restaurant that night. I just wanted to give them back their data but when I saw the party…"

Cade closed his hand over Rafe's clenched fist where it lay on the bed. "I know," he said gently. "But you didn't see what I saw that night or in the weeks since Dom and Vin found out you were alive. They were there physically but that was it."

Rafe removed his hand from Cade's, his fingers shaking as he put his own coffee down next to Cade's on the nightstand.

"I can't forgive them," he grated out.

Cade sat up and wrapped his arm around Rafe's waist and drew him against his body. He was glad when Rafe's breathing remained even. "I know, baby."

"I thought it was what I wanted for so long but now that it's done I just wish I could take it back." Rafe's arm curled around his neck and he felt him bury his face against his neck.

Cade dropped a kiss on Rafe's head and said softly, "Will you come with me? I want to show you something."

~

*R*afe felt his limbs go numb when he realized where Cade was taking him. *Barretti Security Group* stood out in dark letters against a white background on the sign leading to the garage.

"Cade, no," he managed to get out as the familiar panic began to overtake him.

Cade had the car parked in the underground garage within seconds and he grabbed Rafe's head between his gentle hands and said, "Look at me, Rafe."

Rafe managed to open his eyes.

SLOANE KENNEDY

"They're not here. They're both up in the San Juans," Cade said firmly. "It's Saturday so there will hardly be anyone here. Trust me, please."

Rafe took in deep breaths until he felt the fear start to fade. He felt his body relax and he leaned back in the seat. The panic attacks were coming way too often. Even when he'd been selling his body night after night, he'd never been wracked with this level of anxiety this often.

"Good?" Cade asked and Rafe realized Cade was holding his hand, their fingers intertwined. He nodded and Cade released him so they could both get out of the car.

What Cade had said turned out to be true as they stepped into the executive suite. It was deathly quiet as he followed Cade to a big office overlooking the Sound. A massive mahogany desk sat against one wall and in the middle of the office was a seating area complete with a leather couch and several comfortable looking chairs. There was even a small bar with a refrigerator and along the back wall he saw a door that led to a bathroom.

Cade pulled out the leather desk chair and sat down, his gaze going to the dual computer monitors. He punched a couple of keys on the keyboard, then maneuvered the mouse around. After a couple of clicks he stood and pulled the chair out for Rafe.

Rafe sat and looked at the screen in confusion. His eyes finally lit on a networked folder with his first name on it.

"When you searched Dom and Vin's personal files, did you ever look for your name?"

Rafe shook his head. The thought hadn't even crossed his mind.

"Take your time," was all Cade said as he suddenly headed for the door. He stopped in the doorway and said, "I'll be down the hall in the breakroom if you need me." With that Cade closed the door and Rafe was alone to stare at the folder. He took a deep breath and double-clicked it and his eyes widened as hundreds and hundreds of additional folders appeared, all with dates on them. His gut clenched as he opened the first one and began reading.

~

*R*afe's fingers trembled as he scrolled down what had to be the hundredth document he'd scanned through. He heard the door open and expected to see Cade checking in on him again as he'd been doing every twenty minutes for the last two hours. But it wasn't Cade.

He watched in stunned silence as Dom entered the office and closed the door behind him. He didn't even notice Rafe until he was almost a dozen steps in. When he did finally look up, Rafe wasn't sure which of them was more shocked – him at the stunning physical transformation that his brother had undergone since the last time he'd seen him or Dom at seeing his baby brother sitting at his desk.

"Rafe," Dom said in a harsh whisper.

Cade's description rang in his ears as Rafe looked Dom up and down. He really did look like a zombie. Pale, sallow skin. Dark smudges under his pain filled eyes. Hollow cheeks, slumped frame. Guilt swept through Rafe at knowing he was the cause of all this. His one-time hero was nothing but a shell of a man.

"I wasn't stealing anything," Rafe said quickly as he stood, the desk chair sliding across the floor with his hasty move. "Cade let me in."

Dom shook his head, his wide eyes never leaving Rafe. "It's okay."

They both stared at each other for a long time, the awkward silence between them a living thing.

"You have her nose," Dom suddenly said and Rafe winced when he realized Dom was referring to their mother. Dom seemed to realize what he'd said too because he paled even more. "Sorry."

Rafe reached up to touch his own nose before he realized what he was doing. "I don't really remember what she looked like."

"There's a picture behind you on the credenza," Dom offered.

Rafe turned and found the picture Dom was referring to. It was of their mother and all four boys. He assumed his father, or Dom's father rather, had been the one to take it. He skimmed his fingers over his mother's image and then studied each boy in turn. Vin with his broody countenance, Ren with a wide smile and Dom...Dom with his then skinny arm wrapped around Rafe's shoulders.

Pain went through him and he quickly put the picture face down. At least maybe now he'd see the mother from this picture rather than the one that had lived for so long in his head – the one where she lay unmoving on the kitchen floor as blood sprayed over her unseeing eyes and lifeless features as her body jerked every time the butcher knife was plunged into her chest.

"Rafe," Dom said softly and Rafe snapped his head up. Dom hadn't moved at all but from the worried expression on his face he guessed that Dom had noticed he'd been getting lost in the past.

Rafe needed to get this done so he could get out of here.

"I didn't know," Rafe murmured as he turned one of the computer screens so Dom could see. He knew what Dom was looking at because he'd spent the last two hours combing through the endless folders going back to the week Gary had taken him and ending the week Rafe had revealed his identity to Cade in the club. Each folder held notes and letters from private investigators, lawyers and social workers from all over the country.

"I just wish it had been enough," Dom said, his voice breaking.

"You must have spent hundreds of thousands of dollars," Rafe said.

Dom shook his head. "We would have given anything, Rafe. Would have paid anything for even one lead."

"You have hundreds of files on different Gary Prices all over the country."

"After he took you we searched all the addresses he'd filed with the court and social services. The ones that weren't fakes were dead ends. We couldn't even figure out what state he had taken you to. Once we could afford it, we hired PIs all over the country to track down guys named Gary Price who fit Gary's general description but nothing ever panned out. We tried adoption agencies and foster care in case he gave you up at some point. Eventually we started checking with morgues..." Dom said, his voice cracking.

"He told me you were glad he'd taken me," Rafe whispered.

Dom shook his head vehemently but Rafe continued before he

could speak. "I didn't believe him at first. But as time passed it was all I had to keep me going. Anger made it possible to get through each day when hope couldn't. I let it consume me and turn me into someone I don't even recognize anymore. I shouldn't have let things get this far," he admitted.

"Please, Rafe, it's not too late," Dom said desperately.

"It was too late the second he took me," Rafe managed to get out. His whole body began to shake as he stepped around the opposite side of the desk.

"Rafe?" he heard Cade call from the doorway. A shiver of relief went through him knowing the man he needed more than anything at this moment was nearby, but he shook his head slightly when Cade made a move to come to his side. He returned his attention to Dom.

"I told Cade earlier that I couldn't forgive you," he began. Dom physically stepped back as if Rafe had struck him so Rafe hurried on. "But that was before I realized there was nothing to forgive. One man alone is responsible for tearing our family apart. Not you, not Vin, not me. But I can't be around you and move forward. That bastard tied you to a part of my life I want to forget," Rafe said as his voice broke.

Tears fell down Dom's face and he watched the briefcase he'd been carrying slip unnoticed to the ground.

"I need one thing from you, Dom."

"Anything," Dom said instantly.

"I need you to move forward too. I need to know that I didn't do to you what Gary did to us."

Dom wiped at his tears. "You didn't. I have so many amazing people in my life and I won't let anyone take them from me. Never again."

"You'll tell Vinny?" Rafe asked.

Dom nodded. "I'll tell him. We'll be here whenever you're ready to come home, okay?"

Rafe couldn't manage to respond so he forced his legs to move, giving Dom a wide berth as he focused his gaze on Cade.

"Rafe, please don't do this," Dom suddenly whispered as he passed.

But Rafe steeled himself and kept moving as tears slipped down his face.

"Gary Price. Is he still alive?" Dom asked from behind him, his gravelly voice threaded with anger now.

"No," Rafe managed to get out just before he reached Cade and felt a big hand close over his. A guttural sob tore through the air as the door closed behind them and he had no idea if it had come from him or his brother.

~

"You coming to bed?" Cade asked as he settled his hand on Rafe's shoulder.

"Soon," Rafe muttered as he clicked on the mouse beneath his palm over and over again.

It had been like this for two weeks and Cade was at a loss as to how to deal with it. Ever since his meeting with his brother, Rafe had been a madman when it came to trying to find out who was after him. The hours that he wasn't desperately fucking Cade into the mattress were spent in front of his laptop. Even Eli's visits failed to drag Rafe away from the computer.

Whatever emotional connection they'd managed to establish the night Rafe had left the apartment to go to Logan's foundation had started to fray. The sex was still amazing and left them both drained with pleasure but there'd been something missing. Rafe hadn't been dismissive or selfish in any way in bed and he never left Cade to return to his own bed but it was like he went somewhere else in his head – somewhere that Cade couldn't reach him.

Watching Rafe's encounter with Dom had nearly destroyed Cade because it hadn't been his intention to push the brothers into a confrontation. He'd just wanted Rafe to see that his brothers had never given up on finding him. But his intent had backfired and Rafe seemed more desperate than ever to get away from them…him.

Cade slammed the laptop closed and when Rafe opened his mouth to complain, he fused their mouths together. His gamble paid off and

Rafe melted beneath him as his arm reached up to wrap around Cade's neck. When Rafe stood, Cade backed him up until Rafe's legs hit the bed.

"Cade, I don't have any stuff in here," Rafe said as Cade pushed him down onto the bed.

"We won't need it," Cade answered as he pushed Rafe's shirt up. As Rafe worked the shirt off, Cade ran his tongue over the flat, brown nipples and then licked his way up to Rafe's armpit. He'd discovered the erogenous zone a couple of weeks ago and it never failed to drive Rafe crazy with need.

Fingers grabbed his shoulder to hold him in place but Cade was on a mission and he dragged himself lower, his lips and teeth searching every bit of exposed skin. When he reached Rafe's jeans, he had them off easily and was pleased to see the man had foregone underwear. He didn't give Rafe any warning as he opened his mouth wide and drew Rafe's cock down his throat in one swallow.

Rafe jackknifed up to a sitting position and rammed his hips forward as his hands closed over Cade's head. But this was Cade's show and he let Rafe's length fall out of his mouth as he reached up with his hands to grab both of Rafe's wrists. He used his whole body to push Rafe back down on the bed and kissed him hard and deep as he pinned his hands to the bed. He was glad when he didn't feel any fear at the gentle restraint. Releasing Rafe's lips, he muttered, "Keep them there," as he glanced at Rafe's hands. He bit back the smile that went through him at Rafe's quick nod.

Cade worked his way back down Rafe's body but bypassed the dick that bumped his cheek as Rafe shifted his hips in desperation. He reached down and grabbed Rafe's legs and pulled them up so his heels were resting on the edge of the bed and Cade dropped to his knees.

"Cade," Rafe whispered, a hint of fear now in his voice.

He looked up and made sure his gaze connected with Rafe's. "Trust me," was all he said. Rafe hesitated for only a moment before he nodded once more.

Cade used his hands to pull back Rafe's cheeks and once again, he gave Rafe no warning. He closed his mouth over Rafe's opening and sucked gently before letting his tongue flick over the pulsing hole.

"Fuck," Rafe shouted. Cade grabbed Rafe's legs before he could move them and began licking Rafe in earnest. Rafe moaned but didn't fight him. In fact, he shifted his ass further off the bed so he was even closer to Cade's mouth. Cade took that as an invitation and used his hands to lift Rafe's ass off the bed so he could get a better angle. He felt Rafe shift and glanced up to see that Rafe had wrapped his hands around the backs of his knees to make it easier for Cade to reach him.

Cade slurped all around Rafe's entry and then sucked hard. As Rafe moaned and writhed with every touch, he stiffened his tongue and pushed the tip inside Rafe's heat. Rafe shouted at the contact and then began pleading with Cade not to stop. He gave Rafe a few more licks and then jammed his finger into his own mouth to cover it in saliva. He quickly replaced his tongue with his finger and when Rafe stiffened, Cade leaned forward and sucked Rafe's dick into his mouth.

"Yes," Rafe moaned and suddenly he was pushing down on Cade's finger, forcing the digit all the way inside. Cade kept up the intense suction with his mouth as Rafe thrashed on the bed and he felt Rafe's legs press against his shoulders as the man sought more leverage. Cade matched the thrusting of his finger into Rafe's ass with the drags on his cock. He used his free hand to massage Rafe's balls and could tell by how tight and drawn up they were that Rafe was near the edge.

Cade curved his finger inside of Rafe till he hit the gland he was looking for and just like that Rafe began shooting into his mouth as he screamed Cade's name. Endless jets of semen coated his tongue and throat as Rafe's body clamped down on his finger and he released Rafe's balls so he could reach into his own pants and finish himself off.

When Rafe finally settled as tiny aftershocks went through him, Cade gently removed his finger and licked up the little bit of come that had missed his mouth. He dragged himself up and over Rafe's body and was glad when Rafe instantly opened his mouth to him and kissed him heartily.

"You okay?" he murmured against Rafe's lips.

Rafe just nodded and wrapped his arms around Cade, dragging him down for another long kiss.

"You play dirty, Cade Gamble," Rafe said softly.

"Hell yeah I do," Cade responded before he settled his whole body down on Rafe's and kissed the shit out of him.

CHAPTER 8

*R*afe tensed at the knocking on the front door. Cade had left an hour ago for the office and Eli never knocked but just let himself in with the code. Not to mention it was only nine in the morning. But whoever it was would have needed a code to get in the building not to mention permission from the burly security guard who sat at the front desk in the lobby.

"Rafe, it's Logan," he heard from the other side of the door. Rafe must have waited too long because Logan said, "I'm not here about Dom."

Rafe opened the door, stiffening his resolve at the sight of his brother's lover. He didn't look much better than Dom had two weeks ago.

"Can I come in?" Logan asked.

Rafe stepped back and nodded his head. He followed Logan to the living room but didn't sit on the couch next to the other man. It occurred to Rafe that they should get a second piece of furniture for people to sit on. A shot of horror went through him when he realized he'd just thought of himself and Cade as a "they" and the comprehension was so disturbing that he ended up sitting on the couch anyway.

This wasn't his home. Cade wasn't his. God, he needed to get a fucking grip. He'd spent two weeks running himself ragged searching his files for any clue of the threat that had yet to materialize again and fucking Cade senseless night after night as their impending separation loomed. Because there would be a day when he would need to walk away from Cade. What they had was great sex and they got along well enough but it wasn't enough to base a future on, let alone ask the guy to leave his family. If only Cade hadn't shattered him last night...

"You okay, Rafe?"

Rafe shook the image of Cade kneeling between his legs out of his head. He managed a nod.

"Constance showed me the mock-up of the website you did. I was hoping you could get it up and running for us as soon as possible."

Rafe nodded again, not sure why the hell he couldn't find his voice. Because he was still stuck on the fact that he'd thought of himself and Cade as a couple.

"I was wondering if you might take a look at our network. We've been having some issues with the wireless signal and I'm not sure if the security is as good as it could be. We keep a lot of private information about our donors on them."

"But can't Dom..." Rafe began but stuttered to a halt at the pang of loss he felt go through him.

"Dom's been pretty preoccupied lately and he's got a lot of catching up to do at work since he's been gone for a few weeks now."

A few weeks? Hadn't Dom gone back to work after their encounter?

Logan continued. "I spoke with Cade this morning before I came over and he's willing to bring you down to the office tomorrow to take a look."

He absolutely should say no. He was trying to distance himself from these people.

"Okay," he heard himself say. And to his horror his mouth kept moving and he whispered, "Is he okay?"

Logan studied him for a moment. There was no condemnation

like he would have expected. "He's doing as well as can be expected," Logan hedged.

The explanation would have to be enough because he had no right to ask for details. Rafe climbed to his feet, suddenly feeling very shaky. Logan seemed to get the hint and stood and Rafe led him to the door.

"Would you tell your sister and your friend I'm sorry for ruining their party?"

"Savannah and Shane don't care about that. They were worried about you. Everyone was."

"Why? They don't know me," Rafe blurted out.

Logan smiled patiently. "Just because you weren't around didn't mean you haven't been part of the family," Logan said. "Dom and Vin talked about you all the time. Ren too."

Logan must not have noticed his look of surprise because he went on talking. "Dom loves to tell the story of you running around the neighborhood completely naked except for a red cape and your super-hero underwear when you were six and your poor mom running after you down the street."

He remembered that. His mother had been yelling at him to stop but he'd told her there were bad guys he had to catch and kept going, ignoring all the startled looks he'd gotten. It had been Vin and Dom who'd found him six blocks over asking a police officer where all the bad guys lived.

"I asked him to move forward, Logan," he said softly.

"He's working on it, Rafe. It will just take him a little bit of time." Rafe nodded and Logan reached for the doorknob. "Would you do me a favor?"

Rafe hesitated to answer but it didn't stop Logan.

"Go easy on Cade. He's the one who's going to be alone when all this is over."

Rafe sucked in a harsh breath and shook his head. "We're just-"

Logan raised his hand to stop him. "I saw the way he looked at you at that party. Whatever is happening between you two isn't "just" anything for him."

With that Logan was gone, leaving Rafe to ponder his confusing statement.

~

Cade pushed open the door to Dom's office. As glad as he was to see Dom behind his big desk, the faraway look on Dom's face said the man wasn't seeing the computer screens in front of him.

"Dom?" he said quietly, not wanting to startle the other man.

Dom looked up at him and then looked around the room as if just realizing where he was. He'd never known his friend to be this out of it and it truly frightened him. What if Dom didn't bounce back from this?

"Hey, come on in," Dom said as he leaned back in his chair.

"Good to have you back, boss," Cade said as he dropped down into one of the chairs on the other side of Dom's desk. Dom smiled at the nickname he hated but it didn't quite reach his eyes.

"How is he?" Dom asked.

"Hanging in there," Cade said. "He's frustrated that he hasn't made any progress with figuring out who's after him. He finally agreed to let me give his laptop to Desi. Hopefully she can offer a fresh perspective."

"Any sign of the threat?"

Cade shook his head. "I decided to go ahead and put someone on my place when I'm not there, especially now that I know Rafe might get it in his head to leave without warning."

Dom nodded. "Can I ask what's going on between you two?"

Cade sighed. It was just a matter of time before the big, protective brother came asking what his intentions were. "I'm not just fucking around with him, Dom. I wouldn't hurt him like that."

Dom studied him for a moment. "It's not him I'm worried about," he finally said.

The observation caught Cade off guard and he shifted uncomfortably. "What do you mean?"

"I don't know him well enough to know how he feels about you. But I can tell he isn't like the others for you. I hear it in your voice."

Cade studied him for a long time before he finally answered. "You're right, he isn't like the others. I'm not the same when I'm around him but I like that," he admitted. "But I don't know what any of it means. I'm completely clueless when it comes to this shit."

Dom smiled. "I don't think you give yourself enough credit, Cade. I remember a time when you saw something between me and Logan that neither of us could admit to."

Cade dropped his eyes to study his hands. "I may end up having to choose between you and him," he said quietly. Even the thought of having to give up Dom and the rest of his family had his heart aching.

"My guess is deep down you've already made that choice."

He had. He didn't understand it but he had. He wanted Rafe. But the physical wasn't enough anymore. He wanted it all.

"Let me know what Desi finds," Dom said. "Vin said he'd be back tomorrow but between the two of us it's still going to take a while to get caught up."

Cade appreciated the change in conversation because the emotions churning through him were just too much to deal with. "Let me know if you need anything," Cade said as he stood.

"Will do," Dom said. But they both knew the one thing Dom needed was the one thing Cade couldn't give him.

~

*C*ade punched in the code to his door and bit out a curse when it beeped at him. He was so fucking excited to see Rafe that he couldn't manage to get the damn code right. What the hell was up with that? He finally managed to get the sequence right and the door clicked and he pushed it open. As he stepped inside, he scanned the kitchen since it was in his direct view. When he saw that it was empty he searched the living room and sure enough, his man was sitting on the couch. But Cade knew instantly that something was wrong because he was holding his head in his hands and rocking back and forth.

"Rafe?" he said softly as he hurried over to him and dropped down in front of him. Rafe didn't seem to notice his presence until Cade placed his hands on Rafe's knees. "Baby, what's wrong?" he asked as he extricated Rafe's hands from the death grip the man had on his own head. Pain filled eyes lifted to meet his.

"What are we doing, Cade?" Rafe asked.

"What do you mean?"

Rafe just shook his head and then looked around the apartment as if seeing it for the first time. "I can't do this."

Cade tensed. He knew it was just a matter of time before Rafe balked at whatever was happening between them but he wasn't ready for this conversation yet, especially since he couldn't be sure of its conclusion.

"Did something happen today?"

"I think I should go stay in a hotel," Rafe said. "I could pay for someone at your company to keep an eye on things. Or I could just disappear…"

Hurt lanced through Cade and he rose to his feet. "Where is this coming from?"

Rafe dropped his head back in his hands and began rocking back and forth once more. "Logan was here."

"Did he say something?" Cade asked, surprised at the sudden anger he felt towards his friend.

"He came to ask me to help with some stuff at the foundation. He was sitting on the couch and my first thought was that we needed to get some more places for people to sit."

"Okay, we can do that," Cade responded, completely confused.

"Jesus, Cade," Rafe whispered as he rose. "There's no 'we' here. The only thing 'we' have is phenomenal sex."

"It's more than that and you know it," Cade snapped.

"How the hell would I know? I've never fucking done this!" Rafe pushed past him and began pacing. "I know how to manipulate, how to use...how to take. I don't know how to do this!" he shouted as he motioned between them.

Cade forced himself to take a deep breath. "Look at what time it is, Rafe. It's not even five o'clock. I left work early because I was excited to see you," Cade said as he stepped in front of Rafe to get him to stop moving. "Not to fuck you. To see you, to talk to you."

Cade let his hands close over Rafe's upper arms. "Does whatever this is scare the shit out of me? Yeah, it does. I could have easily stuck you in a hotel with one of a dozen bodyguards your brothers' company has on staff but I wanted you here. And the fact that you waited until I got home instead of running tells me you want to be here too."

He was glad when Rafe let him draw him closer.

"Don't let me hurt you, Cade," Rafe mumbled just before he wrapped his arms around Cade's neck.

~

"So just double-click this and press ok," Rafe said as he leaned over the old woman with the huge glasses who had her nose nearly pressed against her computer screen.

"Did I do it?" she asked, her wide eyes lighting up with excitement.

"Yep, it's posted," he said with a smile.

He bit back a laugh when she high-fived him.

"Nice work," Rafe said as he left the woman's desk and went back to the small cubicle Logan had set him up in.

"Did you really just manage to teach Doreen how to post on our blog?" Logan asked as he stepped around the cubicle wall.

"She was already close," Rafe insisted. "She was just missing the last couple of steps."

"How about some lunch?"

Rafe stiffened. Logan had asked him that every day for the past four days he'd been coming to the foundation to help out. He'd managed to beef up the network security on the first day but when Logan had asked him to look at some of the older machines to see which ones needed upgrading, he'd agreed to come back the following day. Every time he'd finished one task, Logan found him another.

And the lunch invites had started on day one. His polite excuse that he wasn't hungry hadn't deterred Logan because he asked again the next day and when he insisted that he had too much to do, Logan approached him again on day three. Whatever awkwardness that should have been between them since Logan's comment about him not hurting Cade, not to mention the bigger elephant in the room, the devastation he'd wreaked on those closest to Logan, seemed not to exist for the young man because he was as kind and friendly as he'd been from the first day they'd met.

"Okay," Rafe heard himself saying and strangely enough, he didn't regret it. He honestly liked Logan. Would they ever be friends? No, not possible. But something inside of him wanted to know more about the man who'd stolen his brother's heart. Worse yet, he wanted to know how Dom was doing without actually asking.

"Great, there's a Chinese place down at the market. Sound good?"

Rafe nodded and stood. As they headed for the front door, Doreen gave him a bright grin and a wave as he passed her desk and he couldn't help but smile back.

"Who do you have with you today?" Logan asked as he pushed open the door. "Hey, Jagger," Logan said before Rafe could respond. They both watched as the behemoth of a man pushed off the wall next to the front door.

"Logan," the big man said with a nod.

Between the bald head, tattoos on both arms and the giant scar that slashed across one cheek, Jagger was a scary looking guy. He wasn't a big talker either though that didn't seem to bother Logan at all.

"Okay if we head down to the market for some lunch?" Logan asked.

Jagger nodded and waited for them to pass before he fell in step behind them.

Cade had spent the first day keeping an eye on him when he'd arrive at the foundation bright and early but had agreed to let Jagger take over when Rafe insisted he go back to work. Cade had resisted at first but when Rafe had admitted that Cade's presence was too much of a distraction, Cade had smiled arrogantly and kissed him hard. That had led to an intense make out session in Cade's car in the garage of his building which had been followed by Cade being bent over the couch as Rafe fucked him. They'd managed to get through dinner and half an action movie before they were on each other again.

Rafe heard Logan chuckle next to him.

"What?" Rafe asked.

"I know that smile," Logan said.

Rafe hoped like hell he wasn't blushing because he definitely felt the heat rising in his cheeks. They didn't speak again until they'd placed their orders and were sitting at a small table against the window of the main building that many of the market place's shops were located in. Jagger had refused Logan's invitation to join them and instead sat near the entrance, his eyes constantly on the move as people came and went around them.

"Where'd you learn all the computer stuff?" Logan asked as he took a long drink from his soda.

Rafe tensed. He knew it was a completely legitimate question but since his upbringing had been anything but normal, even the simplest of inquiries were challenging.

"I took a few college courses but I found the pace to be too slow so I ended up teaching myself mostly."

"Why hacking?"

Man, no holds barred with Logan.

"I think at first it was just the challenge aspect of it. I started chatting with other hackers online and they began linking me up to potential customers. Mostly just stealing intellectual property from competing companies."

He expected recrimination but Logan just nodded. "Dom loves the computer stuff but it's all gibberish to me."

Rafe stiffened at the mention of Dom but Logan just continued on. "He tried explaining to me what was so impressive about the way you hacked their system but he lost me after two minutes."

"If it makes him feel better, it took me a lot longer to get through their firewall than most places." Rafe realized what he said and wanted to smack himself. But Logan just laughed.

"I'll be sure to tell him that," Logan said.

"No, don't," Rafe said.

Logan sobered. "He's doing okay, Rafe. I'm not going to lie and say it's all sunshine and roses but he'll find a way to make peace with what's happened. Vin too."

"I'm glad they have you guys," Rafe admitted.

"I can't speak for Mia but God knows I'm the one that got lucky. I pushed Dom away so many times that sometimes I still can't believe he forgave me."

"Why'd you push him away?" Rafe asked, his curiosity piqued. He knew the facts that were on paper but they told little of the actual story.

Their waitress appeared with their food and Logan waited until she was gone to respond.

"I'd never been with a man before," he admitted. "Hadn't ever been attracted to one."

Rafe nearly spit out his food.

"He'd also just lost Sylvie so I was struggling with that too."

"Sylvie was his wife?"

Logan nodded. "She had leukemia. She lost her battle with it a month after I met them."

Rafe knew from the information that he'd stolen that Dom had paid Logan to spend the night with him and Sylvie.

"It's okay, Rafe. You can ask. I'm not ashamed of it anymore."

"You were with them both," was all he said.

Logan nodded. "I began escorting when I was in college to support myself and my sister after our parents died. I kept doing it to try and build my business – the space the foundation is in used to be my bar. It was supposed to just be another job that night but there was something about both of them that drew me in. I tried to ignore my feelings but Sylvie saw something in me that I didn't. She saw it in Dom too. She's the only reason we found each other," Logan said quietly.

"But the reason we're together now is because Dom loved me enough to forgive me for the pain I caused him."

"So you named the foundation after her?"

"I named it after her because she reminded me how important it was for people to have hope. Meeting Eli made me realize that kids like him were the ones that needed it most but usually had the least."

They both ate in silence for a moment before Rafe found the nerve to ask, "How'd you know Dom was the one?"

"I knew when being apart from him hurt more than the shame and guilt I was feeling over how we had come together in the first place. He always put me first, even before himself."

The food became harder and harder to swallow so Rafe finally put down his fork. Was that what Cade had been doing? Putting him first? The small, sweet gestures? Giving up control in bed because it was what Rafe needed?

"How'd you get over your past?" Rafe asked softly.

"I guess I really don't think of my past as something I had to get over. I had to learn to accept some of the decisions I'd made because they made me who I am. I suppose it took meeting Dom to see the good instead of just the bad."

Rafe was too lost in thought after that for any more conversation and Logan must have sensed it because he didn't press Rafe to talk anymore. It wasn't until they were back in front of the foundation that Rafe finally snapped out of his reverie.

"Hey Cade," he heard Logan say.

Rafe looked up to see Cade leaning against his car. A smiled tugged at his lips at the sight of the gorgeous man watching him so intently.

"Can I steal him away a bit early today?" Cade asked Logan though his eyes never left Rafe. Something warm bloomed inside of him.

"You bet," Logan responded. Before Rafe could even process what was happening, Logan gave him a quick hug. "Have fun," Logan whispered against his ear before releasing him and disappearing inside, leaving him alone with Cade. He had no idea if Jagger was still around because he only had eyes for Cade.

"You up for a little vacation?" Cade asked as he reached out his hand and pulled Rafe against him.

"Yes," Rafe said without hesitation.

"Good," Cade said softly before leaning down to brush a kiss over his lips. "Let's go."

CHAPTER 9

*V*acation turned out to be a weekend trip to Friday Harbor on San Juan Island. When Cade had first mentioned going to the San Juans, Rafe had immediately feared it was some type of trick to get him in the same room with Dom since Dom owned a house on the island. Then he'd immediately felt guilty for thinking the worst because Cade hadn't pressured him even once to try and mend fences with Dom and Vin. He hadn't even mentioned either brother after the traumatic run in with Dom at his office.

By the time they settled into their room at the Bed and Breakfast, they'd both been too tired from the long trip to do anything besides eat a quick dinner and fall asleep. There'd been no sex, yet it had been one of the best days of his life. Just getting out of the city had been a relief but to have Cade laughing and joking with him as they made their way north to the ferry terminal had been a unique and exciting experience. The man had a wicked sense of humor. He'd also been up front about Jagger being behind them and that he would spend the weekend trailing them. Having another set of eyes on things seemed to relax Cade even more so Rafe was more than okay with the arrangement.

If he'd had any hope of spending the weekend in bed with Cade though, he'd been sadly mistaken because Cade woke him up early the next morning. But he'd made up for it with a toe curling blow job followed by a repeat performance in the shower that left them leaning hard on one another in an effort to stay upright. The rest of the day had included a whale watching tour, kayaking and a stroll through the many shops in the small, touristy haven. A huge seafood meal at a quaint little restaurant overlooking the harbor had been followed by gelato from a small ice cream shop. And on the walk back to the Bed and Breakfast, Cade had held his hand, not caring who was watching.

"Did you have fun?" Cade asked as he unlocked the door to their room.

In answer, he dragged Cade's mouth down to his. He finally released Cade and said, "That was my first date." He brushed another kiss over Cade's lips. "I'm wondering how you'll ever be able to top it," he murmured.

Cade smiled against his mouth. "Does that mean you're going to put out?"

"You bet your ass it does," Rafe said with a laugh.

~

Cade fell back on the bed as Rafe sucked him deep. The man's mouth was truly sinful. Gentle fingers rolled his balls back and forth as a tongue licked from his base to his tip and then back again. It was a great way to end what had been a perfect day. Watching Rafe smile and laugh had unfurled something deep inside of him that he hadn't even known was there. And he no longer had any doubts whatsoever. He was completely and totally in love with Rafe Barretti.

As Rafe worked his way back up Cade's body, he felt the drag of Rafe's clothes against his heated skin. He reached for the buttons on Rafe's shirt but Rafe grabbed his arms and pinned them down next to his head. A thrill shot through him at Rafe's show of dominance and when Rafe sent him a no nonsense look before releasing his hands, Cade left them where they were. As Rafe took his time working the buttons of his own shirt free, Cade groaned as Rafe's jeans rubbed against his cock where Rafe was sitting astride him.

The shirt finally disappeared but Rafe shook his head when Cade made a move to reach for him. Rafe humped slowly against him as he unfastened the button of his jeans and then lowered the zipper but then he climbed off Cade entirely. Worse yet, he left the fucking jeans on while he reached his hand into them and began stroking himself. Cade had to crane his neck to watch and saw that his own cock was turgid and leaking and every time Rafe dragged his hand up and down his own dick, more fluid dripped out of Cade's cock.

"Rafe," he whispered. There was no humor in Rafe's eyes as he studied Cade's shaft but the lust that was there was something to behold. Rafe finally pulled his cock free of his jeans.

"Turn around. Hang your head off the bed."

Cade did as he was told and bit back a moan when Rafe stepped up to him and ran his cock over Cade's lips. "Open," Rafe ordered.

But he didn't push into Cade's mouth right away. He just kept teasing around it and Cade finally let out a groan when a drop of Rafe's tangy fluid hit his tongue. He closed his mouth long enough to fully enjoy the flavor and as soon as he opened, Rafe was shoving into him, the angle allowing him to hit the back of Cade's throat in one easy stroke. As Rafe began thrusting into him Cade reached around Rafe to grab his ass. But when Rafe leaned over him and sucked his dick down, Cade shouted around the shaft that had him impaled.

It took him a second to gather his wits but then he was catching up to the rhythm Rafe set and he added to it by searching out Rafe's hole. When he brushed over the opening, Rafe's suction increased as did the pounding his mouth was taking. His nose was buried against Rafe's groin and he inhaled deeply, the musky scent driving him higher. Rafe's arms wrapped around his thighs as Cade began thrusting his hips up to drive himself further into Rafe's lush mouth. He felt the tingle in the base of his spine that said he was close but he wasn't about to release Rafe long enough to warn him. But Rafe must have sensed it on his own because he pulled off of Cade and trailed his hands up Cade's abdomen and chest and then wrapped his fingers around the base of his own cock and dragged it free of Cade's mouth. A rough, wet kiss followed and then Rafe was pulling him up and positioning him back on the center of the bed.

Rafe worked his pants and underwear off, then got the lube and condom from the nightstand. In seconds he was back over Cade, their cocks lined up. Cade dropped his hands on Rafe's thighs as Rafe worked the condom wrapper open. The muscles beneath his palms bunched as Rafe shifted to put the condom on but he didn't put it on himself.

Cade reached out a hand to grab one of Rafe's wrists – the one holding the unrolled condom over the tip of Cade's cock.

"Rafe, no, you don't have to," Cade said as dark blue eyes met his.

"I want to," Rafe whispered. "I'm ready."

Cade shifted up so that he was sitting and he wrapped his arms around Rafe's waist. "Baby, what we have is perfect. I don't need this," he said as he pressed his forehead to Rafe's.

Rafe brushed a quick kiss over his lips. "I need this," Rafe said softly. Arms went around his neck. "I need all of you."

Cade ran his palms over Rafe's back before pulling back enough to study Rafe long and hard, searching for any signs of fear. Cade had told the truth. What they had was enough for him but to share everything with Rafe had his love for the man in his arms go from a smoldering burn to a full on inferno.

"I love you," he whispered against Rafe's lips and when the man gasped in surprise, he took advantage and thrust his tongue inside and skimmed every surface and crevice until Rafe was squirming against him. When a hand closed around his dick, Cade released Rafe and lowered himself back on the bed. Desperation glinted in Rafe's eyes as he quickly worked the condom on and reached for the lube. Cade could see his declaration had thrown Rafe for a loop but he didn't regret it. And he didn't care that Rafe hadn't said it back because deep down he knew Rafe felt the same thing he did.

Rafe's fingers shook as he slathered some lube on Cade's cock but when he reached behind himself, Cade grabbed his hand. He wiped

SLOANE KENNEDY

Rafe's hand on the bedspread and then reached for the lube. "Turn around."

I love you. Rafe's legs trembled as he turned himself around so that his ass faced Cade. Cade's words of love had taken him completely by surprise and he'd been sure the overwhelming surge of emotion inside of him would lead to a panic attack of epic proportions, but even though his breathing had ratcheted up and he was feeling hot all over, it wasn't even close to the same thing.

He'd made the decision earlier in the day to give himself to Cade completely and he'd expected that at some point he'd chicken out before actually doing it but the overwhelming need to give Cade the gift that Cade had given him so freely had been too much to ignore. Yes, he was scared to death and he hoped like hell he wouldn't back out but he knew that even if he did panic, Cade wouldn't recriminate or judge him for it.

Rafe felt cool air on his hole when Cade gently drew one cheek back. He braced himself for the feel of the cold liquid and blunt fingers but what he got was heat as Cade's tongue licked over his opening. The man had done this to him countless times since the first night in the guest room when he'd done his sneak attack and it never failed to drive Rafe insane. He dropped his arms down onto Cade's legs to brace himself and then cried out when a hand stroked down his cock. At this rate he'd be done long before Cade ever got inside him.

"I'm too close," Rafe managed to croak as Cade applied suction before slicking him up with more saliva. Cade took pity on him and gave him one last kiss before fingers replaced his mouth. There was no pain when Cade breached him to the first knuckle, just intense pressure and a slight burning. The cool lube actually felt good against his flaming skin and he pressed back when more of it was pushed inside of him. The move forced more of Cade's finger into him and he winced when his hole finally collapsed.

114

"Okay?" Cade asked as he twisted his finger gently inside of Rafe to spread the lube.

Rafe managed a nod since he didn't trust himself to speak. It felt better than he could have imagined and every time the rough skin of Cade's finger brushed the smoothness of his inner walls he felt a spark of electricity shoot through him. There was more burning and pressure as another finger joined the first and began scissoring inside of him. Cade hit his prostate without warning and a jolt went through his cock and he automatically reached for it and began stroking it desperately.

"Uh, uh," Cade murmured as he pulled free of Rafe and forced his hand away from his cock. "We come together."

Rafe turned around and began to climb off of Cade though he wasn't sure if the man wanted him on his back or his front – he really hoped it was the former because he wanted to maintain the eye contact with Cade so he wouldn't drift into the past. But Cade stopped his movement and held him in place.

"Your show," Cade said as he reached past Rafe and held his cock up. It was then that Rafe realized that Cade, as always, was focused on him. He would get to control every part of this which meant he could stop it whenever he wanted to. Love bloomed in his chest but the words stuck in his throat as he leaned down to sink his tongue into Cade's mouth. He put every part of himself into the kiss and hoped like hell that Cade could feel what he was still afraid to admit.

Rafe pulled back, lifted his hips and shifted back. Nerves skittered through him as he felt the tip of Cade's cock push between his cheeks and seek out his hole. Cade's eyes never left his and Rafe used that as his anchor as he sank further down until Cade's crown breached him. As many times as he'd had Cade in his mouth, the man felt a hundred times thicker and harder and the intense pressure frightened him. Logic told him Cade would fit but he couldn't help but remember how much damage even the smallest dick could cause when used to inflict pain instead of pleasure.

"Rafe, baby, look at me," Cade murmured as a heavy hand came to rest on his chest.

Damn, he'd closed his eyes and lost the much needed connection. But it was there when he opened them again– the strength and love in Cade's intense gaze reminding him who he was with.

"I'm okay," Rafe said as he covered Cade's hand with his own. He lifted slightly until Cade nearly slipped out of him and then sank back down, gravity helping him to take more of Cade inside. Rafe let out a rush of air when a few more up and down motions had Cade sliding all the way home. He sat there for a long time and just enjoyed the burning, stretching sensation that began to give way to something else entirely.

"So fucking perfect," Cade whispered and Rafe realized he'd closed his eyes yet again. The look Cade was giving him was raw and hungry and Rafe instinctively twisted his hips, the rough hair at Cade's base brushing against him and bombarding him with more sensation. Cade moaned but didn't thrust into him like Rafe expected. Still putting him first.

Rafe pulled up and slid back down and managed to keep his eyes open this time as pleasure rocked through him. Every time he did it he felt the heat in his body rise and his body draw tight. Within minutes he was grinding helplessly onto Cade as he sought the relief his body craved but it wasn't enough.

He dropped down to brush his lips over Cade's parted lips and whispered. "Take me, Cade. Make me yours."

The words seemed to be all Cade was waiting for because Cade dug his heels into the bed and punched his hips upwards. Rafe cried out and used his hands to push himself upright as Cade set a ruthless pace. He reached for his cock and began dragging his hand up and down it over and over as Cade surged into him. Hands closed around his waist and pulled him down hard on every upward motion.

"Fuck," Cade shouted and then suddenly he was sitting up. He grabbed Rafe's legs and maneuvered them so Rafe's thighs were pressed against his waist and his legs closed around Cade's back and then his hands were back on Rafe's waist as he began slamming into him. Rafe leaned back and braced himself on his hands, changing the angle enough that Cade nailed his gland with every plunge. The pressure on his arms became too much and he fell back onto the mattress between Cade's slightly spread legs as the other man yanked him further up into his lap and onto his cock again and again.

Rafe managed to get his hand back around his cock but it only took a few tugs before his vision began to dim and his body drew unbearably tight. He screamed as he came hard and he locked his ankles to try and hold himself against Cade's pistoning cock as it shuttled in and out of him. Cade shouted his name as he began pulsing inside of Rafe and he watched in awe as a look of beautiful agony overcame Cade as he rammed into Rafe a few more times with hard, quick jerks as the heat from his come seeped through the condom and warmed Rafe's channel.

As Cade's orgasm flooded through him, he ran one of his big hands up Rafe's body until it closed over his shoulder and then he was drawing Rafe upright until they were pressed chest to chest. Cade's body continued to jerk and twitch against him, setting off aftershocks inside of Rafe and he wrapped his arms around Cade's back. But for every tremor of pleasure that continued to course through him, all he felt was the soft brush of Cade's mouth near his ear as Cade told him once again that he loved him.

CHAPTER 10

*A*ren't there security cameras in here?" Rafe murmured against his lips as Cade brushed his hand over Rafe's jeans and pressed him back against the walls of the elevator, pleased to feel that even the possibility of being watched didn't deter Rafe's burgeoning erection.

"Yeah," he said. "What do you say we give the security guys a little show?"

Rafe looped an arm around his neck and kissed him soundly and then drew back and smiled at him. "You first," he quipped as he reached for the button on Cade's jeans.

When the elevator dinged, Cade let out a rough curse.

"Guess you should have gotten a place in a taller building," Rafe said with a laugh as he dropped his hand.

"That's gonna cost you," Cade grumbled as he grabbed Rafe's hand as well as their bags and dragged him out of the elevator. He'd never get tired of any of the many sides of Rafe he'd discovered over their too short weekend. Wise cracking, sexy, affectionate, sweet. And still dominant in bed - or the bathroom as it happened to be this morning when Rafe interrupted his morning shave and bent Cade over the sink, shaving cream still covering half his face by the time Rafe rammed into him. The man had smoothly ordered him not to touch his cock and had said all kinds of dirty things to him before he'd come hard and fast inside of Cade. Only then had Rafe turned him around and sucked every last drop from his body.

There still hadn't been any words of love from Rafe but Cade had absolutely no doubt of Rafe's feelings because the minute Rafe had looked down at him last night when he'd taken all of Cade deep into his body, Cade had seen it. The rest of the shit that would be there to greet them on their return to reality no longer mattered. He'd find the threat to Rafe and exterminate it and then he'd follow Rafe wherever he wanted to go. If it meant leaving Seattle behind forever, he'd do it in a heartbeat.

Cade opened the door and let Rafe pass first into the apartment and nearly ran into him when he stopped suddenly, his eyes going wide. Fear coursed through Cade and he grabbed Rafe at the same time that he reached for his gun. It wasn't until he had Rafe behind him and his gun aimed that he realized the threat was in the form of a grim looking Dom and Vin standing in his living room. Anger surged through him that the brothers had used the code he'd given them for emergencies to enter his home without any kind of warning.

"What the fuck?" he snapped as he put his gun away.

He could feel Rafe's hand gripping his tightly and he glanced at him to see that the fun, outgoing lover he'd just been joking with was gone. The only saving grace that kept him from pounding Dom and Vin into the ground was that Rafe didn't seem to be on the verge of a panic attack.

"Sorry, Cade, but we need to talk to him," Dom said softly.

"And you couldn't pick up the fucking phone first?" Cade snapped.

"Cade," Rafe said quietly as he extricated his hand from Cade's hold. Fuck, he could already see Rafe was shutting down emotionally.

"Desi found something," Vin said as he held up a stack of papers. "Just a few minutes, please."

Cade finally nodded and he took Rafe's hand again and led him to the living room. He glanced around and realized Rafe was right - he didn't have enough places for people to sit. He snagged a couple of the bar stools from the kitchen counter and dropped them in the center of the room. The difference in height from the couch would be awkward but it turned out not to be an issue since no one sat anyway. In fact, it ended up being him and Rafe on one side of the room, Dom and Vin on the other. A slash of sadness went through him that this was what their future would be.

"Rafe, Desi found some emails on your computer that we think explain who might be after you," Dom said carefully. He could see the longing in both brothers' eyes as they studied Rafe but Rafe stood stiffly next to him, his eyes heavy with turbulent emotion. Any hope he had that Rafe might be on the path to accepting his brothers died in that instant.

"We know you're the one that sent the anonymous tip about Ren's location," Vin said.

Cade stiffened. Ren had only been found because Vin and Dom had received an email with GPS coordinates that led straight to the caves the terrorists had been keeping Ren in. They'd never been able to figure out where the email had come from.

"It was you?" Cade asked in a mix of amazement and confusion. Why hadn't he said something?

Rafe nodded.

"How?" was all Cade could manage.

It was Vin who spoke. "He hacked the Department of Defense's servers."

Rafe shifted defensively. "I only took stuff relating to Ren. I queried their system for whatever they had on his disappearance."

"Does the name Phillip Benton mean anything to you?" Dom asked.

Rafe shook his head.

"Benton was a liaison at the base where Ren was stationed. You pulled his emails," Vin said.

Rafe nodded. "I hacked the emails of anyone who knew him. I didn't read them – I just searched for references to Ren. I finally found an email where a villager said he'd seen Ren being held in the caves near Bamyan in Afghanistan. The villager said Ren had helped him and his family and that's why he was reaching out with Ren's location."

"That email was sent to Benton but he never reported it to his superiors. In fact, it looks like he deleted it."

Understanding seemed to dawn on Rafe and he slowly sank to the couch. "Even when you hit delete, you're never really deleting anything," Rafe said numbly.

"There were more emails," Dom said as he carefully lowered himself to the opposite end of the couch. "They were between Benton and a woman named Geraldine Holt. She was an aid worker that Ren was having a relationship with."

"But she was using him to steal information on his unit's movements. She and Benton were working together to sell weapons and supplies to the Taliban. The ambush was a set up so the terrorists could get their hands on some tactical weapons Ren and his team were safeguarding during transport," Vin explained.

Rafe dropped his head into his hands and Cade reached down to put a hand on his shoulder.

"Everybody was supposed to be killed that day but we're guessing the terrorists took Ren and his surviving teammates as hostages so they could try and ransom them to the U.S. for money or use them as part of a prisoner exchange."

"Jesus," Rafe whispered. "I didn't even look at the rest of the emails after I found his location. It didn't even occur to me."

"Benton must have figured out his system was hacked. We don't know how he knew it was you but Ren being rescued by Vin and his men probably was what made Benton suspicious," Dom said.

"It would have been easy for him to find someone to backtrack my hack," Rafe murmured. "There's a hundred guys out there better than me and I was so focused on what I was doing with you..."

Rafe's voice dropped off.

"I contacted some friends at the Pentagon," Vin said. "Benton's in the wind. He took off a few weeks ago and no one's heard from him since."

"You have a picture?" Cade asked, his juices flowing. Finally, a name for the fucker who'd dared to come after Rafe. Who'd left Ren to rot in that hell hole.

Vin nodded and pulled out his phone and sent the picture to Cade's phone. He hadn't gotten the best look at the guy when he'd been shooting at Rafe but one look at the beady eyes and thinning hair that appeared on his phone and he knew.

"It's him," Cade muttered.

Rafe suddenly stood. "I can disappear," he said quickly as he suddenly reached for his bag and headed towards Cade's room. He'd long since moved the few belongings he had into Cade's bedroom.

Cade grabbed his arm. "No, not an option." He could feel Rafe shaking beneath his hand.

"You think he's going to give up, Cade?" Rafe glanced quickly at his brothers. "How long before he comes after you and the people you love just to get to me?"

"We can protect you," Vin said.

Something passed over Rafe's features at Vin's words but it wasn't the doubt or resentment Cade would have expected Rafe to feel after hearing the promise he'd heard once before so many years ago. No, it was longing, concern, fear. He was truly afraid for his brothers and their families...for him. And that worried him because fear could drive even the smartest people to do stupid things.

"You're not leaving," Cade snapped, unconcerned that he was being too aggressive.

"Let go," Rafe said firmly as he tried to pull free.

Cade never took his eyes off Rafe when he said, "Go." Dom and Vin got his message and headed for the door. Cade heard the door close behind him and he released Rafe when he yanked his arm free.

"This is not something you get to decide for me," Rafe snapped as he again started towards Cade's room.

Cade grabbed him once more but this time he backed him up until he hit the foundation beam near the entry way to the kitchen. The same one he'd tied Rafe to that fateful day weeks earlier. He held him gently by the throat as he pinned him with his body.

"You remember the last time I had you here?" he said softly.

He didn't miss the feel of Rafe's shaft pressing against his but Rafe remained silent.

"That was the last time there was a you or a me because I knew the second I held you in my arms in the shower that you were mine and I was yours. There's only "we" now and *we* will make this decision together."

"I don't want you to have to choose," Rafe whispered, his body softening against his.

"It's too late for that," Cade replied as he leaned in and kissed Rafe. Relief went through him when Rafe didn't fight him and kissed him back. Within minutes they were locked in each other's arms on Cade's bed and Cade yanked Rafe's shirt off. He knew he should go slow but the thought of Rafe walking away from had him desperate to bind this man to him. Rafe worked his own pants off as Cade stood and shed his clothes and then he was reaching into the nightstand. He grabbed the lube and settled over Rafe once more who welcomed him by separating his legs so Cade could sink between them.

"I need to be inside you again," he muttered as he skimmed his hands over Rafe's chest. "Nothing between us this time," he said as he held up just the lube. "I've been tested, I'm negative," he said and waited.

"Me too," Rafe said with a quick nod as he dragged Cade back down for another kiss.

"I can't go slow," Cade rasped as he reared back and opened the lube.

"Don't," was all Rafe said, his dark eyes burning.

Cade's fingers shook as he got Rafe ready and when he finally sank inside in one smooth motion, he groaned in contentment. Strong arms wrapped around him as he tucked his hands under Rafe's back and pulled him flush against his chest. Rafe pressed soft, sweet kisses against his lips even as Cade pounded into him. The more urgent Cade's need became, the more Rafe lovingly touched him and spoke soft words of encouragement to him as if to reassure him he was still there. And when those long awaited words were whispered into his ear, Cade came apart and he shouted Rafe's name as he filled Rafe with spurt after spurt of his release. Rafe's fingers bit into his arms as he shattered beneath Cade and liquid heat pooled between them. Cade separated their bodies enough to pull his dick free of Rafe long enough to rub it the white fluid on Rafe's abdomen. He made sure Rafe could see their come mixing together and then he buried himself deep inside of Rafe's body once more and just stayed there as they kissed.

As time passed and Rafe made no effort to separate from him even though he knew the man probably wasn't comfortable with cooling come on his stomach and in his ass, Cade forced himself to pull out.

"Let's take a shower," he said as he ran his hands through Rafe's hair and pressed gentle kisses over his face.

Rafe nodded.

Cade stilled his hands on the side of Rafe's neck and said, "Promise me you won't leave." He kept his eyes trained on Rafe's eyes as the other man studied him for a moment.

"I promise," Rafe said, his eyes never wavering. "I love you, Cade," he said. "More than I thought possible," he admitted and Cade knew he was telling the truth.

"I love you too," he whispered and leaned down to kiss Rafe once more before forcing himself to stand.

"I'll get our bags," Rafe said as he stood and brushed a kiss over Cade's lips.

Cade nodded and went into the bathroom to start the shower. As he waited for it to warm he glanced down at his stomach and smiled at the few specks of Rafe's release that glistened against his skin. He couldn't help but swipe his finger through it and take a taste. He had no idea when he'd become such a hedonist but with Rafe, everything was turning out to be new. And his gut told him that it would be that way for the rest of their lives.

Cade searched the bathroom closest for some fresh towels. All that was left were a few hand towels so he went to his bedroom and grabbed a couple of towels from the laundry hamper. Not ideal but laundry had been the last thing on his mind in recent days. As he turned back to the bathroom, something shiny caught his eye and his stomach fell out when he realized what he was looking at. Rafe's watch – the one he never took off – was sitting on the nightstand.

~

*H*e'd lied. He'd stared into the eyes of the only man he'd ever loved and that loved him back and he'd flat out lied. The words about loving Cade had been true, but everything from the moment Cade had pressed him up against that beam had been a lie. He'd known as soon as Cade admitted that he'd already chosen him over Dom and Vin what would have to happen next. The irony had been that Cade had been the desperate one during their lovemaking while Rafe had savored it because he knew it would be the last. He'd wanted to remember every touch, taste, sound. And when Cade had emptied himself inside of him, he'd nearly lost his resolve to go through with his plan. Even now knowing that part of Cade still lingered in the recesses of his body had him craving more.

But then Cade had asked him to promise not to leave and the old, manipulative Rafe had returned and he'd seamlessly lied straight to his lover's face. It was still easier than having to listen to the way Cade had dismissed Dom and Vin in favor of him. Cade had already started the process of ending the relationships that had made him who he was. Rafe knew what it was like to not have a family. No way in hell would he condemn Cade to that.

Rafe pushed open the stairway door that led into the parking garage and then ran over to the doorway that led to the street. He had no idea if Jagger was still on duty so he'd decided to forgo using the lobby door. He followed the alley up to the main street and checked up and down for any sign of Cade or Jagger but there was no one. It was still light out but there was little foot traffic around. But Rafe knew that would change the second Cade realized he was gone. He had minutes at most so he walked quickly down the sidewalk, his eyes scanning the street for cabs. After dragging on his jeans and shirt on the way to the living room, he'd managed to snag his wallet from his bag on the way out the door but had left everything else behind since he didn't need it.

Within a minute he spied a cab on the opposite side of the street.

"Rafe!"

At the same time, he heard Cade scream his name, tires squealed as he stepped off the curb. Everything after that happened in slow motion. The black sedan barreling at him. A hard body slamming into his. Flying through the air. The sound of cracking glass. And then nothing.

He struggled to take in air as his aching body rolled across the pavement. He finally managed a deep cough and then a shallow wash of air went through his oxygen starved lungs. Another one followed and he rolled onto his back, his eyes staring up at the stormy clouds passing at a snail's pace above him. A shadow passed over him and it took him a split second to realize what he was seeing – a man standing over him, a gun pointed directly at him. A bullet shattered the air around him and he closed his eyes as he waited for the searing pain but there was nothing. When he opened them again, he was face to face with the same man who now lay lifeless on the ground next to him, blood and brain matter seeping from the hole in the side of his head.

Rafe scrambled away from the gruesome sight and looked up to see Jagger hurrying towards him, gun drawn.

"You okay?" Jagger asked as he neared.

"Cade? Where's Cade?" he asked as he frantically searched around, bits and pieces of the last minute rushing back to him now. The oncoming car. A body hitting his, holding it close as the car struck them.

"Cade!" he screamed, his voice dropping off as he finally found him. "Oh God," he cried as crawled the few feet to Cade who lay completely still in a crumpled heap in the middle of the road. Blood trickled from his nose and there were cuts all over his face.

"Cade!" he yelled again as he ran his fingers over Cade's face. But he wouldn't answer. He dropped his head to Cade's chest and sobbed in relief when he heard a shallow breath and a faint heartbeat.

"Jagger, get help!" he called as he reached down to press his lips against Cade's mouth.

"Cade, please, wake up," he begged. "I'm sorry, please!"

Tears streamed down his face as he continued to plead with Cade to respond but there was nothing. Absolutely nothing.

CHAPTER 11

*R*afe wrapped his arms around himself as he focused on his breathing. In and out, just like Cade had told him so many times. He closed his eyes and let Cade's touch float over his skin as his deep voice counted the seconds between breaths. Everything around him disappeared as Cade brought him back down. There was no hard waiting room chair beneath him, no overhead speaker calling out for doctors to go to certain rooms, no people shuffling past to get to the vending machine for their hundredth cup of coffee. It was just him and his man.

"Rafe?"

A palm settled on his upper arm but it wasn't the right one. The voice was wrong too, but he knew whose it was. Had never forgotten it in the twenty years since it had promised to bring him home.

Rafe forced his eyes open and saw his brother's concerned face as he knelt in front of him. Vin was standing right behind Dom and beyond that he could see Jagger talking on his cell phone.

"He wouldn't wake up," Rafe whispered brokenly just before he launched himself into Dom's arms. Dom somehow managed to pull them both to a standing position and then he was holding Rafe tight.

"He's strong, Rafe," Dom whispered against his neck.

When arms wrapped around him from behind he completely lost it and began sobbing. His keening cries sounded foreign even to his own ears but neither Dom nor Vin tried to stop him or settle him in any way. They just held him. At some point they managed to get him into a small, quiet room but Rafe was too far gone to care how and when. He was sitting on some type of bench and leaning against Dom who had an arm wrapped around his shoulders. Vin was sitting on a chair directly in front of him, his hand holding Rafe's in a near death grip.

"I left," Rafe blurted out. "I thought it would be better if I disappeared," he whispered. His eyes stung from the pain of fresh tears falling. "He put his body between me and the car. He took the brunt of it."

"He needed to protect you," Vin said gently.

"He…he had a seizure in the ambulance," Rafe managed to get out as the image of Cade convulsing uncontrollably on the gurney flashed through his mind. "They said his brain was starting to swell and they had to relieve the pressure…" He struggled with remembering what the doctor had told him as they took Cade away from him. "They have to do a cran…cran…"

"Craniotomy," Dom supplied.

"He's tough, Rafe. And he's got something to fight for so he's going to make it, do you hear me?" Vin said firmly as he shook his hand.

Rafe had no idea if he nodded or not but it was the last any of them spoke for a long time. When the door to the room opened and a doctor entered, he jumped up as his heart leapt into his throat.

"How is he?"

The doctor glanced at him in confusion and said, "Are you Mr. Barretti?"

He was too keyed up to correct the doctor about his last name so he just asked, "How is he?" again.

"Mr. Barretti, I'm just here to take a look at your injuries."

Rafe wanted to scream that he didn't give a fuck about his injuries but a gentle hand closed over his shoulder.

"Rafe, Cade's going to want to know you're okay when he wakes up," Dom said softly.

He had to give his brother credit for using Cade to get his compliance. He managed a stiff nod and followed the doctor to another room full of medical equipment. As the doctor motioned to the bed he heard Dom say, "We'll be right outside, okay?"

Panic began to sift through Rafe. He didn't want this man touching him. He just wanted Cade. His brother must have seen something on his face because Dom hesitated at the doorway and then moved back into the room. He came to a stop in front of Rafe and then gave him a reassuring squeeze on his arm as he nudged Rafe towards the hospital bed. "Just keep your eyes on mine, okay?" Dom whispered as he went and dragged over one of the chairs along the far wall so that it was directly across from him.

"Would you remove your shirt, please?" the doctor asked softly.

Rafe's fingers shook as he began working the shirt off and his breathing started to increase.

"Are you all right, Mr. Barretti?" the doctor asked in concern.

Dom stood and motioned something to the doctor and then focused his attention on Rafe.

"Did Cade tell you about how we met?" Dom asked.

Rafe shook his head as he tried to suck in more air. "He said you were in Iraq together."

"We were but we were in different units. I was heading back to my bunk one night and some guys started hassling me. One of them was a soldier I'd messed around with, but I'd told him to fuck off when I heard him saying some pretty nasty shit about an officer who'd been transferred out because he admitted to being gay. Don't Ask, Don't Tell was still in effect at the time," Dom said as he stepped back and sat back down in the chair.

Rafe felt his shirt being raised and fingers skimming over his shoulders and then down his chest and between his ribs.

"So it was seven to one," Dom continued. "I was getting my ass kicked and then out of nowhere this giant of a man steps in and knocks two guys out before anyone even realized he was there."

A smile skated over Rafe's lips at the image.

"I didn't even have to lift a finger because the last two guys took off running when he finished off three more guys by himself." Dom laughed. "Then he steps over one guy and asks me if he can bum a smoke. When I told him I didn't smoke he starts searching the guys he'd just beaten the shit out of."

"I didn't know he smoked," Rafe said as his breathing started to normalize. A stethoscope was placed on his chest and he inhaled deeply when the doctor asked him to.

"He's been doing it off and on for a long time but he finally quit for good earlier this year," Dom answered.

As the stethoscope traveled to his back, he sensed the doctor pause. He hoped to God the man didn't ask about the scars because he didn't really want Dom to see them. Luckily the doctor continued his examination and then drew his shirt back down.

A disturbing thought went through Rafe and he asked Dom, "Were you and he ever..."

"No," Dom said quickly as he shook his head. "Just friends."

Rafe nodded, thankful there wouldn't be yet another reason for weirdness between them.

The doctor interrupted with several questions as he finished up his exam. Rafe wasn't thrilled to hear he'd need stitches for a gash on his cheek but at least they'd be done with the benefit of numbing drugs instead of liquor this time. Tears threatened again as he remembered the stitches Cade had done on his arm – the ones after the first time he'd saved his life.

"What if he doesn't make it, Dom?" he heard himself asking.

"He will," Dom said firmly, his tone brokering no argument.

Dom stayed with him while the stitches were put in and just as the doctor finished up, another doctor entered the room, Vin right behind him. Rafe jumped off the bed when he recognized the stern looking man as the one who'd told him Cade would need surgery.

"How is he?" Rafe asked before the doctor could even introduce himself.

"He's stable," the doctor responded and the rush of relief that went through him was so powerful that his knees actually buckled and Dom's bracing arm was the only thing that kept him upright.

"He made it through surgery and they're taking him to the ICU now. He broke his leg in two places and he's got a couple of cracked ribs but obviously the head injury is our biggest concern."

"Can I see him?" he whispered.

The doctor nodded. "I'll have a nurse take you up once they have him settled."

It was Vin who asked the question Rafe couldn't manage to get past his lips. "What are his chances?"

The fact that the doctor hedged brought all of Rafe's worries back to the forefront.

"We won't know the extent of the damage until he wakes up. Hopefully that will happen in the next twenty-four hours," the doctor explained.

But Rafe stopped listening at that point because he could only hear what the doctor wasn't saying – that Cade might not wake up at all. He felt himself being dragged against Dom's chest once more and he didn't even bother to try and stem the tears that fell and soaked quickly through his brother's shirt.

~

*T*he week that followed was the worst in Rafe's entire life. The brutality he'd suffered as a child didn't even come close to the torment of watching Cade fight for his life. He hadn't woken up as doctors had hoped and another seizure had the ICU doctors putting him into a medically induced coma. Seeing Cade's lifeless body surrounded by tubes and machines had wiped out all the courage Rafe had managed to muster up before entering the ICU and it was only Dom and Vin who'd managed to keep him on his feet long enough until they found a chair for him that they placed next to Cade's bed. Touching Cade's warm hand had helped but as day after day passed with no change, Rafe grew more and more despondent. But he'd staunchly refused to leave Cade's side even to sleep and he'd shoved away any food that was brought to him.

By the third day it had been Vin who'd physically dragged him out of the room and ranted at him for not taking care of himself and only the reminder that Cade would be pissed to see what he was doing to himself had convinced Rafe to go home with Vin long enough to shower and eat. He'd ended up falling asleep on the short ride to Vin's house and hadn't even fully woken up when Vin somehow managed to get him into the bed in his guestroom. When he'd awoken, he'd been frantic with worry but Vin had sworn that there'd been no change and that Dom and Logan would stay with Cade until he got back.

He'd spent nearly all his time at Cade's side talking to him about inconsequential things and the few times he'd been left completely alone with Cade, he flat out begged and pleaded with Cade not to leave him. His brothers and their loved ones had taken shifts staying with him and most passed the time telling him stories about how they'd come to know Cade. At first it had hurt because he was too raw to deal with the emotion of it but as the days passed, the stories soon became like a lifeline for him. And the sheer number of people who cared about Cade and viewed him as an equal member of their dynamic family unit had him realizing how much he'd been missing out on for not even considering trying to reestablish a connection with his brothers.

And his brothers...

They'd done exactly what Cade had said they would and welcomed him with open arms. And as they stayed by his side day after day and literally picked him up when he was too weak to go on, the image of watching them standing helplessly by as Gary pulled him to his waiting car began to fade.

By day seven the doctors began the process of bringing Cade out of the coma and yet another waiting game started. He didn't even realize he'd fallen asleep until a hand closed over his shoulder and gently shook him. He snapped into a sitting position and whipped his head around to see if some miracle had occurred and deep green eyes were staring at him but nothing had changed.

He turned back to see who it was that had woken him and saw Cade's friend Jax smiling down at him.

"Hey, I can sit with him if you want to stretch your legs for a bit," the big man offered.

Rafe shook his head and scrubbed a hand over his face. "I'm okay, thanks."

Jax pulled up another chair and sat next to him. He didn't know much about the former FBI agent turned country cop who'd shown up the day after Cade's surgery. But like the rest of the people who loved Cade, he'd kept a nearly twenty-four-hour vigil.

"How you holding up?" Jax asked.

What could he say? That a little piece of him died as every hour passed and Cade slipped further away from him? So he just shook his head and remained silent.

"I'm glad he found you, Rafe."

Rafe dropped his head and laughed harshly. "He's here because of me. Every time he gave, I took. Every time I was weak, he was strong. He was willing to give up the only family's he's ever had to be with me and what did I do? I ran. I lied to his face and I ran. And even then he was still willing to risk his life to save mine."

"Why'd you run? I've known Cade a long time and if he chose you it was because he wanted you more than anything else."

"I was afraid..." Rafe admitted.

"Afraid of what?" Jax asked gently.

"That I wouldn't be enough for him. That he'd resent me some day." Rafe looked down at his hands as he clenched them together. "I spent so many years not tying myself to anything because I didn't want to risk losing it. No house, no friends, no future. I could survive losing him while he still loved me but to have to watch what he felt for me turn into something ugly...I wouldn't have been able to put myself back together after that."

Rafe lifted his eyes to look at Jax. "I need another chance to show him I can put him first for a change."

"Hey asshole," Jax said and Rafe's mouth opened in shock. It was then that he realized Jax wasn't looking at him when he spoke.

He turned and clamped his hand over his mouth to catch the sob that threatened to escape when he saw Cade watching him.

"Fuck off," Cade managed to rasp out with a faint smile, but his eyes stayed on Rafe and when Rafe closed his fingers over Cade's hand, Cade managed to squeeze it back.

"I'll get someone," he heard Jax say behind him.

Rafe couldn't stop the harsh cries that overtook him and he leaned down to carefully place his head on Cade's chest, mindful of the wires and tubes that still protruded from the man's battered body. He was too overcome to speak but he knew he didn't have to when Cade's hand gently came to rest on his head. There'd be plenty of time for words later.

EPILOGUE

*C*ade leaned back against the supple leather seat as the sun warmed him. The motion of the car was soothing as Rafe carefully maneuvered in and out of traffic along the busy streets of Anacortes. He could tell Rafe was nervous by the endless drumming of his thumbs on the steering wheel but he couldn't blame him since this afternoon was a pretty big deal for him. It would be the first time he experienced the entire extended family in a social setting since the disastrous night he'd shown up at *Barretti's* during Shane and Savannah's engagement party. Although everyone had been at Rafe's side during the three weeks Cade had spent in the hospital, it hadn't exactly been a great "get to know you" time.

"It's going to be fine," Cade murmured as he reached out to put his hand on Rafe's thigh.

"I know," Rafe said quickly – too quickly.

"I guarantee that all eyes are going to be on that kid," Cade said. Logan's best friend Gabe and his wife had welcomed a daughter into the world two weeks earlier and Dom and Logan were throwing a party for the new parents at their house on the island.

"I didn't exactly make the best impression last time everyone got together for a celebration," Rafe reminded him.

"Believe me, our family doesn't give a shit about impressions," Cade said.

Rafe smiled and Cade was glad he didn't argue his use of the word "our" when he mentioned family. Rafe had been making slow but steady progress with Dom and Vin over the past month and had even started doing some consulting for a few of BSG's clients at Dom and Vin's request. But Rafe's true passion lay with Logan's foundation and he spent most days there or at the first satellite location that had opened earlier in the month.

"How are you doing?" Rafe asked as he glanced at Cade with concern. "Your leg bothering you?"

Cade shook his head. The cast had finally come off earlier in the week which he was supremely grateful for since it made it much easier to move around and also because it meant he could finally fuck Rafe in any position he wanted to. Not that he didn't mind Rafe riding him but having the man screaming and writhing beneath him as he bent him over the bed and pounded into him was something he'd been dreaming of since the doctor had finally given them the okay to resume sex. Not to mention it was incredibly awkward for Rafe to ream his ass when there was a cast that stretched from his ankle to his thigh to deal with.

It frustrated Cade that he remembered nothing of the day Benton had tried to run Rafe down. He'd gotten the nitty gritty details from Jagger – the ones Rafe had been reluctant to share in detail not only because he still harbored a ridiculous amount of guilt for the incident, but because it was hard for him to even talk about seeing Cade after the car had struck them. The aftermath of waiting to see if and when Cade would wake up had also been difficult on Rafe and he'd been glad as hell to hear that Dom and Vin had been there to take care of him.

The physical toll Cade's condition had taken on Rafe had been disturbing to see in the days after he'd woken up but it was the emotional aspect that his lover was still coming to terms with. In the early days after he'd been released from the hospital, Rafe's hovering had been hard to deal with because no amount of words could convince Rafe that he was okay. The man didn't even sleep through the night because he was waking himself up every hour to make sure Cade was still breathing. Thankfully Rafe's worries had eased some and they'd manage a degree of normalcy once Cade finished his rehab and started going back to work and Rafe volunteered at the foundation. Rafe's panic attacks had dwindled considerably and he was usually able to bring himself down before they spiraled out of control.

One area Rafe hadn't held back in was telling Cade how much he loved him and how often. It was something he would never tire of hearing and Rafe backed it up with the way he made love to Cade night after night. There were still the rough displays of dominance that Cade loved but there was everything in between from urgency to sweet to achingly slow and long.

The car rolled to a stop as Rafe parked in line at the ferry terminal. Cade could see the big boat docking so he knew they had a little bit of a wait until they boarded.

"Come here," he whispered as he closed his hand around Rafe's neck and dragged him against his body and sealed their mouths together. Their kiss quickly turned too heated for a public area so Cade forced himself to release Rafe. But Rafe himself didn't seem to be ready to break off all contact because he ran his fingers through Cade's hair – his still short hair. Rafe's eyes darkened when he encountered the scar that ran across Cade's scalp but he seemed to shake it off and his eyes warmed over again.

"Do you think you'd want to marry me someday?" Rafe suddenly asked and Cade sucked in a sharp breath. When he realized Rafe was completely serious he felt a wide smile spread cross his lips.

"Name the day," Cade said.

Rafe laughed and then quieted as he continued to stroke Cade's hair. "Would you take my name?" he asked.

Cade knew Rafe had a list of former aliases a mile wide so he grinned and said, "Which one?"

"I was thinking Barretti has a nice ring to it," Rafe answered.

"I like the sound of that," Cade said.

"Me too," Rafe whispered just before he kissed him.

It was long overdue but Rafe Barretti had finally come home.

The End

ABOUT THE AUTHOR

Dear Reader,

As an independent author, I am always grateful for feedback so if you have the time and desire, please leave a review, good or bad, so I can continue to find out what my readers like and don't like. You can also send me feedback via email at sloane@sloanekennedy.com

Join my Facebook Fan Group: Sloane's Secret Sinners

Connect with me:
www.sloanekennedy.com
sloane@sloanekennedy.com

ALSO BY SLOANE KENNEDY

(Note: Not all titles will be available on all retail sites)

The Escort Series
Gabriel's Rule (M/F)

Shane's Fall (M/F)

Logan's Need (M/M)

Barretti Security Series
Loving Vin (M/F)

Redeeming Rafe (M/M)

Saving Ren (M/M/M)

Freeing Zane (M/M)

Finding Series
Finding Home (M/M/M)

Finding Trust (M/M)

Finding Peace (M/M)

Finding Forgiveness (M/M)

Finding Hope (M/M/M)

The Protectors
Absolution (M/M/M)

Salvation (M/M)

Retribution (M/M)

Forsaken (M/M)

Vengeance (M/M/M)

A Protectors Family Christmas

Atonement (M/M)

Revelation (M/M)

Redemption (M/M)

Non-Series

Letting Go (M/F)